Seb studied her with a long look.

She was so different from him. "I think you're hitting the high nineties—life-percentage wise—if it's okay to say." He watched a heat rise to her cheeks that had nothing to do with the Arizona sunshine. It felt good to compliment her, and she deserved it. "Kent's a great kid and Kimmy is downright adorable. You'll make it through fine."

She laughed. "Oh, I've heard so many versions of those words in the past year. I want to believe them, you know? But I'm not so sure."

It was so easy to see the strength in her she couldn't see for herself. "I am."

"Why?"

"Don't know that I can say." He let himself hold her gaze for a moment before adding, "It just is."

He pulled himself away from the warmth of her company and headed back to the safety of his kitchen. Kate Hoyle was getting to him, and he wasn't sure at all what he ought to do about that.

Allie Pleiter, an award-winning author and RITA® Award finalist, writes both fiction and nonfiction. Her passion for knitting shows up in many of her books and all over her life. Entirely too fond of French macarons and lemon meringue pie, Allie spends her days writing books and avoiding housework. Allie grew up in Connecticut, holds a BS in speech from Northwestern University and lives near Chicago, Illinois.

Books by Allie Pleiter

Love Inspired

True North Springs

A Place to Heal
Restoring Their Family

Wander Canyon

Their Wander Canyon Wish
Winning Back Her Heart
His Christmas Wish
A Mother's Strength
Secrets of Their Past

Matrimony Valley

His Surprise Son
Snowbound with the Best Man
Wander Canyon Courtship

Visit the Author Profile page at LoveInspired.com for more titles.

Restoring Their Family

Allie Pleiter

LOVE INSPIRED
INSPIRATIONAL ROMANCE

LOVE INSPIRED®
INSPIRATIONAL ROMANCE

Recycling programs
for this product may
not exist in your area.

ISBN-13: 978-1-335-58622-3

Restoring Their Family

Love Inspired
22 Adelaide St. West, 41st Floor
Toronto, Ontario M5H 4E3, Canada
www.LoveInspired.com

Printed in U.S.A.

And he said unto me, My grace is sufficient for thee: for my strength is made perfect in weakness.
—*2 Corinthians* 12:9

And he said unto me, My grace is sufficient for thee: for my strength is made perfect in weakness.
—*2 Corinthians* 12:9

Chapter One

Kate Hoyle tried to ignore her son's sour attitude as he carried their cooler toward the kitchen at Camp True North Springs. "Why do I have to come?" Kent moaned.

"Well, we ought to meet the cook, and I can't carry this all by myself."

"Is the cook lady nice?" Kate's daughter, Kimmy, asked, picking raisins from the small box Kate had just given her.

"The camp chef is a man. His name is Sebastian, I think."

Kent lugged the cooler like an annoyed gorilla. "Is he gonna get it? What Kimmy needs?" He nodded toward the little pink backpack Kimmy was wearing. The one that went with her everywhere. The one with the medical information and the EpiPen that always had to be nearby. Always.

"I've already sent all our information on ahead and they sound very helpful. I'm sure we'll be fine."

Kent shot her a dark look far too grizzled for a ten-year-old. Everything left Kent unimpressed since Cameron had died. Grief over his father's death seemed to have locked him into a permanent state of bad-natured apathy. Even the top bunk in their charming little guest room here at the camp left him unimpressed—and she'd thought he would love that.

The one thing that had remained in Kent's nature was the fierce way he protected his baby sister. In fact, that protective air had only strengthened since Cameron died. As if Kent had decided the world was out to do his family in and he'd better stand in the gap. That seemed too great a weight to hoist onto ten-year-old shoulders.

And yet, it wasn't so far from the truth. It wasn't fair how some part of protecting Kimmy fell to Kent now, but what about their lives had been fair lately? Kate simply couldn't do it alone. Most days she felt like she could barely do it at all. At three years old, Kimmy couldn't spot dangers or advocate for her own needs. Kate sorely missed the second set of eyes and ears Cameron had been to keep his daughter safe. Guilt at having to lean on Kent pulled at her nearly every day, but what other choice was there?

We can't have lost the boy he used to be forever, can we? She missed the funny glint that used to shine out of his dark brown eyes. It had been so long since she'd seen the smile that used to show up so often between his freckled cheeks and above his father's handsome square jaw.

It isn't just Kent, she thought as they reached the steps of the main house's wide front porch. Camp True North Springs was built on the family estate of Mason Avery, with a collection of rebuilt outbuildings gathered around a big central house where the kitchen and dining room gathered everyone for meals. *We're all so far from who we used to be.*

Wasn't that why she was here, at Camp True North Springs? To see if they could somehow find their way back to the people they used to be? Yes, she knew losing Cameron had changed them all forever, but there had to be a way for them all to feel more alive, less damaged beyond repair.

"Are there ponies?" Kimmy asked as

she worked her way up the stairs. She was small, even for a three-year-old, and the steps seemed almost half as tall as she was. She had her father's intense eyes but Kate's delicate features—all currently lit up with the optimism her son lacked.

"'Fraid not." A deep voice came from behind the screen door ahead of them. A tall man in a work shirt with a denim apron around his waist and a dish towel over one shoulder pushed open the door. "But we just had a litter of kittens."

Kimmy's eyes popped wide open. "Kitties?"

"Cats," Kent groaned. "Wow. We *never* see those at home."

Kate sent the stranger an "I'm so sorry" look, but Kent's impolite crack didn't seem to faze him.

The man asked, "How about tarantulas? Got those back home?"

That stopped Kent in his tracks. "Tarantulas? Like the giant spider kind?"

The man reached his hands out for the large bag of groceries Kate was holding. He struck her as handsome enough to get away with the dark and dismissive air he carried—someone confident enough, or jaded enough, to not care much what people thought of him. "Relax," he said to Kent's startled look. "I'm just kidding you. Mostly. They're around, but they're way more scared of you than you are of them. They're actually kind of interesting, once you get to know 'em."

Kent made short work of getting the cooler through the door. "No thanks."

"Sorry," the man said, leaning in toward Kate. "I'll dial it back from here on in." Then he hunched down to Kimmy's height. Kate thought she saw him flinch as he bent down, but that could've just been the physical therapist in her forgetting she was supposed to be on vacation. "I'm guessing you're Kimmy Hoyle. I'm Chef Seb. We're gonna take amazing care of you while you're here."

"This is kinda heavy," Kent reminded from ahead of them.

Chef Seb rose again, and there was most certainly a flinch Kate saw. *Leave your professional self in Pennsylvania*, she chided herself. He pointed through a wide archway. "Dining room is in there, and the kitchen is beyond that."

Kate took a moment to look around as Kent disappeared through the arch, mumbling something she was probably glad she couldn't hear. "What a pretty place."

"It is. We've got gardens and benches and a pond that's just coming back from the long drought we had a ways back. There's lots of stuff to do—or not do." He added an over-the-top wink before saying, "And I hear the food is out of this world."

No shortage of confidence here. She gave Seb a tolerant smile. "I'm looking forward to our vacation." Today was Sunday, and she had three weeks of someone else doing the cooking and housekeeping ahead of her. Not only that, but the chance to breathe while someone else gave Kent and Kimmy something fun to do. It sounded like just what she needed. And it didn't matter much if the food was good. It mattered that they were taking her concerns seriously.

That didn't always happen. She wouldn't have come if she'd felt they wouldn't take Kimmy's allergies seriously. It would be so very nice to be able to let down her guard— even just a bit—somewhere other than home. To trust someone else to cook for Kimmy. For-get any exotic vacations—if Camp True North Springs gave her a breather and just the tini-est dose of encouragement, she'd be thrilled.

Kent came back to stand in the archway, looking unhappy. Well, unhapp*ier.* "Mom, everybody eats all together."

"We do," said Seb. "Mason Avery, the guy who owns this place—I'm sure you talked to him—thinks it's important."

Kate could see where this was heading. She had to admit the idea rose a jolt of panic in her as well as in Kent. She kept a tight grip on Kimmy's hand as they walked into the large room filled with big oval tables. Tables too big for a family to sit by themselves, which meant she'd be dining close to other people.

"He didn't mention this. I may need to talk to him."

Seb pushed out a breath. "Well, I have no doubt he'll hear whatever you have to say, but I wouldn't have that conversation...just now."

That didn't sound very accommodating. "Why ever not?"

The chef made an apologetic wince and scratched the tough-guy scruff on his chin. "Well, actually, he and Dana are sort of on cloud nine at the moment. We were expecting you two hours from now."

She didn't see what that had to do with anything. "Cloud nine?" What was that supposed to mean?

"Mason proposed to Dana about an hour ago. You'll have to excuse them if they're a bit smitten, but they're amazing people. Everything will still run like clockwork even if they do have goofy grins on their faces. It's sweet. I'm happy for them."

It was absurd—and rather small of her—to begrudge the two people who ran this camp such happiness. Still, the thought of being around all that love-struck optimism when this camp was all about healing from grief— could she handle it? Had she withered that much? Was she that petty a person now?

Seb tried to salvage the awkward moment. "Mason built those tables. Made them especially for our dining room. Like I said, he feels eating family style is important. It pulls people together. And I really think we'll do it in a way that makes you feel safe."

People didn't understand how severe Kimmy's allergies were. They didn't understand how one small slip could create an emergency. "I don't know…"

"I got all your emails." He was trying to reassure her, but it wasn't working. "I read everything you sent. I've even done research on my own. We are peanut-free for your entire stay. Foods with eggs and milk will have special labels that should be easy to see since we serve family style. No shellfish, either. There will be Kimmy-friendly versions of everything. Even the ice cream. I had our supplier bring in a dairy-free version just for her." He offered Kimmy a smile and then fixed Kate with a deep, steady look. "We're going to take good care of Kimmy. And Kent. And you. You've got my word on that."

Seb caught his breath. *Wow.* Despite her small size and delicate features, this mom was *fierce*. She probably had to be, the way her guard went up like a castle wall at the thought of eating near another family. He had to respect that, even though it probably made his job that much harder.

And still, that was the whole point, wasn't it? All the families at this first trial run of the camp—and probably all the families to come—needed special care. It struck him that this one was going to need an *epic* level of special care. It ought to have irked him, but instead Seb found it pulled a determination from somewhere deep inside him. Helping others was a crucial piece in the addiction-recovery process. He'd come far, but he had a ways to go. Going the extra mile for Kate

Hoyle and her children wasn't just for her good, but hopefully for his as well.

And for the good of the curly-haired cutie currently staring up at him with eyes as sweet as her mother's. Seb's back told him he shouldn't attempt another hunch down, but he did give her another grin. "Strawberry's your favorite, right?"

The sound of her giggle was downright adorable. "Yup."

"I'm not comfortable eating at a table with other families." The mom's tone was miles from calm. He had little hope of diverting her off whatever threat she viewed family-style dining to be.

Someone with your history of recklessness has no business judging wounded people, he reminded himself. Mason had told him he could never forget that, and to reflect a respect for the enormity of their losses in everything he did. People didn't come here because they were okay. They came because violence and tragedy had hacked their life to bits, and they were struggling to pick up the pieces. They were here to rediscover their true north after grief and loss knocked them far off course.

And he, of all people, knew what it was like

to stray so far off course you weren't sure you could find your way back. So that epic level of compassion had better start now. He put all the warmth in his tone he could muster. "It's Kate, right?"

He was glad to see her face soften a bit. "Yes. And that's Kent."

"Kate, Kimmy and Kent. That's a lot of *K*s." He regretted the attempt at humor immediately. *Hello? Tone it down, Costa.*

"Our dad was a *C*," Kent defended. "His name was Cameron."

Seb noted how Kent used "was."

Each of the four families coming today had a loss in the family. So for this family, it was Dad. "We lost him a year ago January," Kate explained. Her voice had a heartbreaking mix of fresh grief and been-at-it-far-too-long endurance. She was what most people would call naturally pretty, with light blond hair in a short cut he normally wouldn't find attractive, but it showed off a pair of spectacular dimples and stunning eyes. She had the kind of creamy skin that didn't need makeup, but whatever glow she'd once had was dragged down by weariness. "It's why we're…here."

She said it like an apology, as if she hadn't

earned the respite Seb and the whole staff were ready to work so hard to give her. To all of them. They'd earned it with the highest price possible, hadn't they? He'd driven himself off track in his life, but they'd made no such choice. Life yanked them off without asking permission.

"It *is* why all of you are here," Seb said, trying to voice the compassionate mission that had drawn him to Camp True North Springs in the first place. "And I mean it. I'm gonna take good care of what Kimmy needs," he repeated.

"You *have* to," Kent practically commanded.

Unlike his mother and sister, Kent must have favored his father, because the boy had dark hair and deep brown eyes. And eyebrows that rarely did anything but furrow in annoyance. His all-too-young bleakness struck a sympathetic chord with Seb. *Been there, kid. Crawling back out of it is no picnic.*

Seb turned to face the boy. "I get it. And I will."

Looking at the sharp set of Kent's shoulders, Seb found himself wondering what it was like to be the "other" child in this family. The one who didn't require a battalion of accommodations. It must be hard under good circumstances, and Kent Hoyle didn't look like he'd seen much in the way of good circumstances lately. *Start here, start now.* "But you get to eat, too," he said to Kent. "What do you like?"

"Me?"

It cut into Seb's chest that the boy looked surprised to be asked. "Yeah," he replied. "We can't let Kimmy have all the fun. What should I cook for you?"

Most kids could name their favorite foods in a heartbeat. This one had to think about it. That said a lot, didn't it? "I dunno… Pizza? Only…the cheese…"

"Oh, I hear you," Seb replied. "Some of that dairy-free stuff tastes more like Styrofoam." He'd tried a few in preparation for Kimmy's needs and found them sorely lacking. "But since I have to make lots of pizzas, I can make sure we have a few you like. Let me guess—pepperoni?"

Kent brightened a little. "Yeah."

"And I'm guessing mushrooms are a no go." Seb loved mushrooms on his pizza, but most kids wouldn't dream of it.

"No, sir." Kent let loose something close to a laugh at that. *There you go. There's a kid in there somewhere.*

"Just Seb'll be fine. Or Chef Seb—I like that, too. So…" He rubbed his hands together in a "let's get started" gesture as he led them toward the kitchen. He wanted to show Kate the supplies he'd brought in and the precautions he'd put in place in the kitchen. "Pizza's your favorite? No others?" He pushed open the double swinging doors that stood between the dining hall and the house's newly expanded kitchen. He hoped the gleaming clean of the place impressed this mom. It was important she felt safe—she and her daughter.

But Kent needed care, too. He was more hurt than he'd ever let on—a guy with Seb's history of falling apart could recognize that sort of armor. "We got three weeks here. That's over twenty meals to choose."

"I really like chili," Kent said with a tiny hint of enthusiasm.

Bingo. "Oh, great choice. There's a million ways to make chili. We can do a lot of things with chili while you're here." He planted his hands on the big stainless steel prep table. "So now there's only one thing to ask. How spicy do you like it?"

While Seb would peg most kids for the milder versions, Kent won his heart by saying, "Really spicy. Like, 'make my lips hurt' spicy."

Kate shrank back a bit as if the mere talk of spicy chili might harm Kimmy's delicate innards. "He gets *that* from his father."

Even better. He could indulge the boy's favorite and honor his lost father at the same time. Seb held up a hand for a high five from the boy. "Man after my own heart. You and me are going on a chili adventure while you're here." He felt compelled to add, "Mom approved, of course."

"But *you* don't have to eat it," Kent chimed in toward his mom. For the first time there was a spark of light in the boy's eyes.

"I won't. Count on it," Kate said. Seb was glad to hear a tiny hint of humor in her voice. That grip she had on Kimmy eased up, too.

Kimmy pointed up to the photograph of Seb's grandmother he'd hung over the pantry. It was a classic shot of Nonna looking like the queen of cooking, hovering over a load of simmering pots. "Grannie?"

"Yep," he replied. "That's my *nonna*. She taught me to cook. I was just telling her how happy I am that camp's starting today."

"She's here?" Kent asked.

"No," Seb said, reaching up to touch the

edge of the frame even though it sent a spike of pain down one side. "She's passed. Two years now."

"So she's gone?" Kent said that final word with a heart-wrenching weight. *Gone.* Everybody who would come here had someone *gone.*

"Yeah, but I still hear her voice in my head. And I guess I occasionally talk back." Only, Nonna hadn't gone in the way these kids had lost people. Nonna had died peacefully in her sleep, surrounded by her family. The families that came here had someone yanked from their lives by tragedy or violence. There was a big, whopping difference in that.

Seb didn't like the way the air hung solemnly on lost family. "I forgot to ask *you*," he said, brightening his tone to address Kate. "What are your favorite things to eat?"

"Mom doesn't have favorites," Kent said. That was a telling remark, too.

"Oh, now, come on—everybody's got favorites." Seb tried to hold Kate's gaze. "Here's your chance. In fact, let's not even bother with anything as boring as main dishes. Tell me your favorite dessert."

Her hesitation spoke of a long season of denial. Whatever her favorite was, he'd guess she hadn't allowed herself the pleasure of it in a long time. "Lemon meringue pie," she said softly. Her cheeks flushed as if she ought to apologize for the preference. "But I can't have it on account of Kimmy. Eggs and all."

"What do you say we find a way to get you some?" he said. "After all, that happens to be a specialty of mine."

That wasn't anything close to the truth. In fact, Seb had no idea how to make lemon meringue pie.

But he decided right there and then he was going to learn. And it would be *epic*.

Chapter Two

After two more very detailed conversations about Kimmy's dietary needs, Seb had finally convinced Kate things would be under control and sent them to the barn house to finish settling in. Dinner was already thirty minutes behind schedule, but getting Kate to a level of comfort about meals was time well spent. *You started out a bit rocky, but it turned out okay*, he reassured himself. He kidded himself that Nonna was smiling down on his first family encounter as "Chef Seb."

"Chef Seb! Chef Seb! Did you hear? Did Dad tell you?" Charlie Avery, Mason's young son, came barreling into the kitchen.

Seb knew exactly what news Charlie was bringing, but he feigned ignorance just to give the boy the thrill of delivering it. "No. What?"

Charlie grinned. "They're getting married!"

Seb plastered a shocked look on his face and pretended to drop his dish towel. "Who? You?"

The boy laughed, his eyes sparkling with joy. "You know who. Dad and Dana. He asked her before the new friends got here and she said yes. Gave her a real pretty ring and everything." He made a face. "They kissed a lot."

"You get to do that when somebody proposes." Not that he knew. He'd never been that much in love, but Seb had to admit it was heartwarming to watch Mason and Dana. It had been a long time since he'd seen two people so meant to be together. Maybe Nonna and Papa. Certainly not his own mother and father—they fought so constantly, Seb had moved out the minute he could. "Have you met all the new friends yet?"

Seb liked Charlie's insistence that the attending families be called "new friends." The boy's cheery openness was such a poignant contrast to the closed-off and angry air he'd just gotten from Kent. They weren't that far apart in age, Charlie and Kent. And both boys knew what it was like to lose someone to a terrible tragedy. Dana and Mason were part of the official staff of the camp, but Charlie's role here seemed just as important. "Ordained," as Dana liked to say.

Dana had said his own presence here was "ordained" as well. He hoped so, and had said a few prayers that it was the case, but some of the blunders he'd made with Kate made him wonder if he really bought into that. Yet.

"I said hello to Kent," Charlie said, looking out the window of the big kitchen through which you could see one end of the barn turned dormitory. "He was quiet. They all are, kinda."

"Just at first, I hope," Seb said as he began opening bags of shredded lettuce for the session's first dinner of tacos. "Hey, can you test a churro for me? They're over there on the counter. Use the tongs like I taught you. No touching food that isn't yours." One of the adjustments of opening the camp was teaching everyone the difference between a private kitchen and a food service one. Small changes, mostly procedural, but highly important—especially with a "new friend" like Kimmy Hoyle to feed. He was going to give this his all and run the safest, most efficient kitchen Arizona had ever seen.

"Your churros are always good, Chef Seb."

Seb had to admit he rather liked the tiny dose of affirmation he got every time someone referred to him as Chef Seb. It was as if he might finally be stepping into the person he was supposed to be all along.

And he was just as pleased to see Charlie carefully use the set of tongs to select one of the sugary fried dough sweets and bite into it. The boy nodded his approval. "These are great," he proclaimed with his mouth still full.

"Good," Seb replied. "We gotta be sure. It's an important night."

"Sure is," Mason Avery said as he pushed through one of the swinging doors from the dining room. "Big night."

"Been a big day already," Seb called out. He wiped his hands on his apron and came over to give his employer a big hug. "Congratulations, man. Charlie spilled the beans on your big news."

Mason beamed. "She said yes. I'm going to be running this camp with my *wife*." He gave the word a goofy, smitten emphasis. Seb had never entertained even one second of doubt Dana would say yes.

"And me," Charlie piped in.

Seb returned to the giant bags of lettuce. "Should I warn everyone that the three of you are going to be unbearable mountains of happiness for the rest of the week? Maybe the whole summer?" His groan was only a tease—he was genuinely happy for his employers. Mason had been wildly nervous, but no one within a hundred miles doubted Dana would say yes to his proposal. "Are you sure you can spare attention for all the new friends?" *Kate Hoyle's going to need a lot of attention*, he thought.

"Absolutely," Mason said, his dark features lit up with a grin. He turned to his son. "Charlie, can you go see if Dana has things all set up for the game before dinner?"

Once the boy was out of earshot, Mason's face grew more serious. "Dana said you already coordinated things with Kate Hoyle about Kimmy?"

"We're set." After a moment's hesitation, Seb admitted, "But she's really nervous about it. She told me this is the first time she's done any kind of traveling away from home since her husband died. She's not at all on board with the whole family dining thing. I've never seen anybody look so worn-out." He nodded to the counter beside Mason. "Hand me those, will you?"

Mason shook his head as he reached behind him to pick up the tray of bright red tomatoes. "Dana said the same thing. I'm glad she's here for three weeks. I think it will take her that long to even start unwinding the knots."

"I promised her Kimmy won't have a speck of trouble while she's here." When Mason gave him a concerned look, he added, "What?"

"I know you wanted to make her feel better, but that wasn't the smartest promise to make. We can't guarantee Kimmy won't run into a dietary issue while she's here."

The gentle reprimand from his employer grew a knot of its own in Seb's chest. "But she won't," he defended. "I'm going to do everything I possibly can to make sure of it."

Mason pointed at him. "*That's* the promise you should have made to her. It's one of the realities every family here has faced. You can't guarantee outcomes. Even when you do everything just right."

Seb swallowed hard. That was one of the deep truths of Camp True North Springs, wasn't it? He knew a bit of history of each of the four families for this trial run of a camp session. In addition to Kate and her children, there were the Boswells. That family from Washington, DC, whose oldest child had been killed in a campus shooting—they'd done everything to give their son a bright future, hadn't they? Only to have it cut short—exactly the issue Mason was talking about. And he knew a few people down in the town of North Springs who would instantly assume that the Domano family was a product of some inner-city neighborhood. In fact, it was the drunk driver careening through their tidy Boston suburb that took their mother away from them. Wouldn't those same people be surprised to learn that the picture-perfect Caldridge girls had lost their big brother to a drug deal gone bad? Mason was right—every family here knew life offered no guarantees. And neither should he.

"Just pay attention to what you say, and how you say it," Mason said kindly. "You wouldn't be here if you didn't have the right heart for the job. You know this is about a lot more than good tacos."

"I won't let you down," Seb said.

He realized he'd made another unwise

promise as Mason cocked his head to one side and replied, "Just tell me you'll do your best."

Seb felt a wave of doubt surge up, tightening his throat. He'd wanted to be the Camp True North Springs cook since the moment he'd heard about the project. He'd been over the moon when he applied for the job and had been selected. Now, at the moment, he felt dangerously unqualified. He was in far over his head despite any mountain of food service protocols and skills.

"Seb," Mason said, softening his tone. "We're all just figuring this out as we go. Dana can plan all she wants—and you know she has—but it's going to be a bit of a bumpy ride this first time. Every family here knows that, even Kate. The point is that we work our way through it together. And that includes you. We're all taking a chance here, remember?"

Seb was deeply aware Dana and Mason had taken a chance on him. After all, was anyone ever totally free and clear of an addiction? Was even the most successful recovery any kind of guarantee? Seb knew that he'd be managing the pull of the opioid drugs that nearly took his life every day from here on in.

The day he forgot that—or denied it—would be his undoing.

He was trying to view the pain that was his constant companion as God's way of making sure he never forgot or denied what had happened. Some days it was easier than others. Pain was a mighty, relentless foe.

"I'm really glad to be here," he said to Mason. "I mean it."

People said tragedy made you strong and wise if you let it. Mason was living proof of that. The man had lost his wife to a horrible road rage accident. Folks in North Springs said he was pretty much a mess until Dana Preston came to him with the idea to turn this family mountain estate into the camp. The guy—and even his son, Charlie—was what recovery ought to look like. In truth, Seb had taken the job partly because he knew it would do him good to just be around a man like Mason.

Mason clamped a hand on Seb's shoulder. "You're meant to be here. Dana and I knew it from the moment you asked if we needed a cook. And not just because you can cook. It's because you can care." Mason reached for the tongs and snatched up a churro of his own. "The way I see it, the food is just the way you show it."

* * *

Even with the chaos of settling in, Kate found herself surprisingly calm and peaceful as everyone gathered around the firepit. The sunset painted the most amazing colors across the sky, while the lazy crackle of the fire mixed with the warm evening air. The logistics of the day made Kate weary to her bones, and she longed to let her eyes fall shut the way Kimmy's were doing. Her daughter grew heavy in her arms, drowsy and relaxed.

She'd been so nervous about dinner. All those families, all those other children with no restrictions who might not understand—it had sent her pulse skyrocketing. Still, a conversation with Mason—and more reassurances from Seb—had convinced her to sit at the same table as two girls and their parents from Dallas.

No disaster had occurred. In fact, Rose Caldridge and her girls, Tina and Cindy, had gone out of their way to be careful and helpful. Kate could almost call the meal pleasant, and the sisters were adorable with Kimmy and even Kent. The girls had lost an older brother. No one talked about how, yet, but did it really matter? Loss was loss no matter how it came about.

Dana Preston, the tall, efficient woman who ran the camp with Mason, came over to sit beside Kate.

"Congratulations," Kate said, surprised she could enjoy the overflowing happiness in the woman's eyes. It was good to be reminded that happy things still showed up in the world. Who could help but enjoy how much Charlie boasted of his father's happy news? Perhaps it was good to be reminded that boys came in happy varieties as well. After all, Charlie had known a loss as deep as Kent's. *Help me get him on the path to healing, Lord. Make use of our time here.*

"Thank you," Dana said, her cheeks turning a bit pink and her green eyes shining bright. "I can't believe he picked *today*." She stared in a sort of disbelief at the lovely ring now glinting in the firelight.

Seb had been right; the two of them looked ridiculously, blissfully happy, glowing even amid all the tasks of getting everyone settled in. "You don't seem to have missed a beat—I'm impressed," Kate offered. "I was hopeless. Completely unable to work with clients after Cameron proposed over breakfast." Realizing that was insensitive, Kate quickly added, "Sorry. I shouldn't have brought that up. It's your day."

Dana's eyes warmed. "No, it's fine. It's good to talk about them—the ones who've been lost. You can always talk about Cameron here. In fact, I hope you do."

"Thank you." Kate sighed. "People still get uncomfortable when I talk about Cameron at home."

Dana smiled. "Charlie calls that 'squiggly.' That funny feeling you get when people are uncomfortable because of what you've been through. I like to think we're a squiggly-free zone here. Everybody gets it. I hope Kent sees that the other kids get it, too." The woman pulled in a deep breath and looked around the circle of the four families. "That's the whole point of this place, actually."

Kate gazed around the circle, noticing a familiar weariness in the eyes of most of the parents. Wouldn't it be wonderful to lay that down, to learn to breathe again, just for a little while? The four families couldn't be more different—boys, girls, city people, country people, families who'd lost parents and families who'd lost kids—but even now she could begin to feel a comfortable sameness.

"Tell me, do you feel the meal went okay?

Everything was right for Kimmy?" Dana asked.

Kate had to admit her fears were unfounded—so far. "Yes. Thank you. I almost never take them out to eat because it's so complicated. People don't understand how careful we need to be."

"We will. I hope we get to the point where you find it a treat to sit down to meals. Not a threat you have to manage."

Kate yawned. The barrage of things to be managed when traveling with Kimmy was exhausting. "That would be nice."

"Did Kent like the food? Not too many guys turn down a good taco in my experience."

"He did. Ate like a horse, in fact." Kent had downed no less than five sizable tacos.

Dana laughed. "Well, that's good." She twisted on the seat to face Kate. "Seb has an idea he'd like to run by you. It's about Kent. It's a bit unusual, but that's our Seb." Dana rose. "I'll let him explain."

As if on cue, Seb walked into the circle of the firelight with an enormous platter. "Nobody wants these chocolate chip cookies for a late-night snack, do they?" he called.

Kate was sure the yells of "Yes we do!"

would wake Kimmy for sure, but the day had conked her out and she barely stirred.

Seb worked his way around the circle, passing out the cookies until he ended up by Kate. He reached into his shirt pocket to produce a small white bakery bag. "And I made two gluten-and egg-free snickerdoodles for Kimmy, but…"

Chef Seb somehow walked the balance between acknowledging the special attention Kimmy needed without making it seem like a huge burden. Did he know what a gift that was?

"I'm sure she'll enjoy them tomorrow," Kate replied.

Seb held out one of the chocolate chip cookies to her. "These are one of my specialties, too. I'm very talented."

"And very modest." She found herself joking back. Joking? It felt as if it had been years since her sense of humor showed up. "Oh, wait…" she said after taking a bite of a still-warm chocolate chip cookie. "You're not exaggerating. These are amazing."

Seb puffed up with pride. "I know, right?"

She polished off the perfectly crispy-gooey cookie in two bites. "Keep these away from me or I'll need a suitcase full of new clothes by the time we leave."

"Now that's the kind of compliment every chef wants to hear." He spread one hand as if viewing a theater marquee. "Seb Costa, Destroyer of Willpower." He had a nice laugh and an admirably easy way about him. Personality-wise, that was. Physically, her physical therapist training clued her in to much more. Kate couldn't help but notice Seb carried himself with the careful air of someone whose body didn't work like it used to.

She motioned to the chair Dana had left empty beside her. "Dana said you had an idea you wanted to talk to me about?"

"I do." He winced as he lowered himself into the chair. In response to her raised eyebrow of inquiry, he explained, "Bum back. Don't let Kent ever ride a motorcycle. One accident can do you in. I'm grateful the helmet kept my noggin intact, but I messed up my spine five ways to Sunday."

Despite all her promises to leave work back in Pennsylvania, Kate said, "I'm a physical therapist, you know. A good set of exercises can help a lot with that."

He waved the idea off. "Nope. Don't help." He leaned gingerly back in the wooden deck chair. "I'm functional, but that's not the same thing as better." Seb reached for a cookie. "I expect you know that in your line of work."

"You probably could improve with the right protocol." Was she offering to help him? That wasn't a good idea for any number of reasons.

She was almost grateful when he held up a hand in resistance. "Please. You're on vacation. Besides, I'm tougher than I look."

He looked rather tough to her. Dark brown hair that erupted into disobedient waves, a scruff of a beard on his angular chin, and the kind of build that fit disarmingly well into a navy blue T-shirt and jeans. More rebel than chef, truth be told. He gave off the air of a former bad boy who was still trying his cleaned-up self on for size. Maybe that's where the bit of his swagger came from—a shred of appealing self-doubt peeking out from under all that oversize self-confidence.

"So," he said with a teasing formality, "I think we should have a chili cook-off. Give our pint-size grump over there something he knows how to do and a chance to share a bit about his father in the process. And I gotta say, a kid who goes for extra spicy just melts my heart." He put his hand on his chest and gave her a showman's grin.

"You're serious."

"I never kid about food. I'm no expert, but I think it could give Kent a way to connect with some of the other kids. He seems to be a bit of a loner." Seb nodded to Kent, who was sitting on a rough-hewn log bench a few feet away. He did not appear to be doing a good job of being patient with Charlie's barrage of questions.

It was hard to admit, but Seb wasn't wrong. "He wasn't always this way."

Seb's gaze was kind. It touched her in a way she wasn't ready for, and gave her hope that she could trust the way this man would treat her son and his many wounds. "I get it. I think cooking his father's supersecret chili recipe could be a way to draw him out. Will you let me try?"

If this radical recipe idea could bring back the Kent she'd once known, it was worth anything. "Yes," she replied, surprised by how easily the agreement came. "Please try."

Chapter Three

"Isn't she the cutest?" Tina Caldridge turned Kimmy on her lap to grin at Kate. Tina and her sister, Cindy, had been putting all the camp's girls' hair into French braids Tuesday morning. Kimmy didn't have quite enough blond curls—or the patience—for the hairstyle, but they'd managed to get Kimmy's hair into a pair of bouncy pigtails that sat atop her head like mouse ears.

Rose Caldridge gave a heavy sigh as she sipped her iced tea on the porch bench beside Kate. Her daughters bore such a striking resemblance to her it made Kate wonder if Kimmy would favor her so much when she grew to be that age. "That's the first smile I've seen from Tina since David's birthday. Well, what *would have been* David's birthday."

Kate knew that sentiment well. "It still is his birthday. He's just not here to celebrate it." She looked at Rose as Kimmy slid off Tina's lap to play some sort of finger game with Cindy. "Did you celebrate it?"

Rose's shoulders rose and fell. "I don't know that *celebrate* is the word. We sort of… got through it." She took a long sip of her drink, probably to swallow back down the tears that were threatening behind her eyes. "Maybe the next one won't be so hard."

"Do you want to tell me what happened? How?" That final word had become a shorthand of sorts between the families already, standing in for "how the person you loved died." Kate knew from experience that sometimes you really *did* want to talk about it. And other times, you couldn't bear to. There didn't seem to be much logic in which was which—or when.

Rose was quiet for a long while before answering quietly. "Drugs. You could say it was a string of terrible choices, but it mostly boiled down to drugs. I don't think David was even choosing anything on his own by the end. The drugs were choosing for him."

It was so horrible to bury a husband. Kate couldn't even bring herself to think what it must be like to bury a child. Especially under those circumstances. "I'm so sorry. I wish there was a better way to say that, too. You get to a point where those words grate on you, don't you?"

Rose turned and looked at Kate with such a stunned expression of understanding. "Yeah," she said, wiping one eye. "You do." She straightened and cast her eyes over to where the girls were amusing themselves. "People said the most dreadful things. I mean, some were really kind, but every once in a while I wanted to look at someone and say, 'Can you hear yourself? What you just said to me?'"

"Brings out the best and worst in people, my pastor said."

Rose's hands strayed to the high school ring that hung from a chain around her neck. Surely it was David's. "I've spent the last nine months as the walking example of every mother's worst nightmare. Even my friends act differently. They watch their words. They're overly nice. They try to pretend they're not as uncomfortable as I know they are."

"Mason's boy, Charlie, has a name for it," Kate said, remembering what Dana had told her earlier. "The squigglies. That feeling in the pit of your stomach when you know people treat you differently. Or are mean. Or stare."

Rose laughed. "Squiggly. I like it. So, does Charlie have a cure for the squigglies?"

"He does. According to him, you tell them to go away and go find someone who understands." Mason had explained it as a child's version of the whole point of Camp True North Springs. To get away and to find people who understood. Wasn't that exactly what was happening right at this moment? Why she felt the knots between her shoulder blades coming just the littlest bit undone as she sat here?

Rose gave Kate a smile. "I think I just did."

Seb walked by at that moment, carrying an enormous bag of potato chips. "I didn't realize we offered makeovers," he said to the girls.

"Look!" Kimmy said to him, pointing to her pigtails, now adorned with sparkly purple bows.

"Wow!" Seb said with oversize astonishment. "Don't I wish I had pigtails like that!"

"Be careful, they may take you up on it," Rose offered. Kate noticed how the woman's demeanor had eased up even as they talked. There really was something to spending time with people who were walking a similar path of grief. All grief was hard, but there was something distinctly hard about the kinds of losses they'd all endured. Losses that felt unnecessary and avoidable, born of things that shouldn't have the power to crush your world, like hate and rage…and drugs and drink.

Seb raised the bag. "I've got too much to do for that kind of stuff. Teenage boys to feed and all. The snacks alone might sink us."

"Are they back from their hike yet?" Kate asked.

Seb checked his watch. "They're due back soon. Even if they're having a ball, the heat and the altitude will get to them eventually. Mason's careful to start them out slow, so don't worry."

"I'm just glad he went at all." It had taken a lot of convincing to get Kent to go along on the boys' hike today. She dearly hoped he'd had fun or it would take even more convincing to get him to do any of the other activities Mason and Dana had planned.

Seb stepped closer to the bench. "Me, too. He tried to come and hide out in the kitchen with me."

Kate tried to hide her disappointment. She

thought she'd been the one to convince him. "And...?"

"Well, I talked him out of staying back with me. But it was an uphill climb. Not a big outdoorsman, our Kent."

There was something both comforting and irritating in how Seb said "our Kent." On the one hand, she had felt so alone in trying to pull Kent through the valley of his grief. Everyone tried to help in their own way, but it wasn't the same thing. On the other hand, she found the instant connection Kent seemed to have made with Seb a bit unsettling. Kent was vulnerable right now. She had to be so careful where he placed his trust.

"I promised him we'd talk about the chili cook-off when he got back. Is that okay?" Seb asked.

"I thought the art therapy thing was this afternoon. I'm looking forward to that," Rose said. "It sounds interesting."

"Not exactly to Kent," Seb said carefully.

"But he loves to draw," Kate replied. "He's really good at it, too."

Seb shrugged. "Maybe he's not ready for group art. And..." he added reluctantly "...I may have hinted that I could get him out of it if he went on the hike. In the name of chili coordination." When Kate gave him a raised eyebrow, he added, "I guess that was over-stepping. I should have asked you first. I'm sorry."

Truth was, Kent would likely hate an orga-nized arts and crafts project no matter how talented he was or how emotionally helpful it might be. If the last months had taught her anything, it was how a mom had to pick her battles with a ten-year-old boy. "It's okay."

"No, it's not. I just… I've got a soft spot for the kid. I like him. But that shouldn't mean I poke my nose in where it might not belong. You're his mother. This is totally your call."

The thought that Kent would be far hap-pier in the kitchen with Seb than doing art with her stung a little. But these weeks had to be about Kent feeling better, too. She hadn't expected Seb's kitchen to be the place where that happened, but maybe she should run with it. Check up on him, keep an eye out for prob-lems, but run with it. "No, I think it will be fine. I miss his art, though. I'm worried about that. He seems to like you."

"Good to hear that." The slight sparkle in Seb's eyes at that compliment hummed under Kate's skin. "He's a great kid, you know. A bit on the grumpy side, but I can work with that." He winked. "Been known to be a bit of a grump myself, actually."

Kate rather doubted that. Seb was a very likable man. Was it safe to admit that, just in the privacy of her own thoughts? Or was that just the allure of a man who had promised her lemon meringue pie?

"When do I get my promised pie?" She surprised herself with such a daring tease. She hadn't been the kind of person to do that in a long time.

Seb shifted his weight. "Working on that. But I promise you, it'll be worth the wait. A world-class pie, guaranteed." With that boast, he walked back toward the big house and the kitchen he claimed as his domain.

"What'd you do to get a promise of a world-class special pie from Chef Seb?" Rose teased.

"I'm not sure," Kate replied.

Rose watched Seb walking away. "I've got a theory or two based on the way he looked at you."

Kate forced a dark look onto her face. "Keep that theory to yourself, okay?"

When Kent didn't show up after the hike, Seb got worried and went looking for him. He wasn't in the art room, nor was he with Kate.

Seb found him sitting under a tree by the front porch. Shade was at a premium in a climate like this, and the patch of greenery under the large tree was a favorite spot for camp staff.

Seb raised an eyebrow when he realized Kent was fiddling with a pencil and a pad of paper.

The boy was squinting at Franco, the amusing ceramic frog with bulging tin eyes that sat next to a little fountain. It was part of what made the shady space such a pleasant place to sit. Kent cocked his head, then scribbled on the paper. *So maybe just not group art.*

Seb walked up and leaned against the tree. A slight breeze fluttered the leaves overhead and made a set of small ripples on the little pond. "I see you found Franco."

Kent looked up. "That's his name?"

"He's a pretty important guy around here. Did Charlie tell you his story?" At a staff meeting earlier this morning, Dana had shared her frustration in finding ways to get Kent and Charlie together. The boys shared so much in common, and Kent's slightly lost demeanor seemed to call out for a friend like Charlie.

"No," Kent replied, "but he's funny. I like him. But I can't get his eyes right." Seb risked the collection of aches and pains it took to get himself down on the grass next to Kent. The boy responded by showing him the drawing. He'd known enough artistic types to recognize they didn't share their work with just anyone. It seemed a good sign that Kent was sharing this drawing with him.

It was an impressive drawing for someone Kent's age. Kate was right—her son did have talent. "You're pretty close," he said to encourage the boy. "Looks just like him to me. You're good at this. But I think he needs the rest of the fountain around him, don't you?" Kate had mentioned that Kent had stopped drawing. That made this particular picture important, didn't it? A first step back to the boy he was before his father's death?

"S'pose," Kent said.

Seb didn't push. He didn't say anything, just sat enjoying the moment and hoping the quiet would give Kent enough space to keep going. It took a few minutes, but eventually Kent's pencil began to move again. The boy's hands moved thoughtfully, hesitantly across the page. Seb was pleased to see the wide oblong of the cement pond appear, then its collection of tin lily pads.

"Always wished I could do that." Seb didn't have to fake the admiration in his voice.

"Yeah, but you cook. Good. That's something." A cattail sprung up behind Franco in the drawing, as well as a set of spiky leaves. Now Kent had taken the extra step of adding new details of his own, different than the scene in front of him. Seb wasn't any sort of art therapist, but that felt like an important thing. He made a mental note to share this little visit with Mason and Dana.

"Mr. Mason says everyone gets a gift of their own," Seb offered. "I guess mine is cooking. It's kind of like art, I suppose."

"'Cept you can eat it," Kent said, finishing off the detail of Franco's webbed feet.

"There's that," Seb agreed. The drawing gave him an idea. "But you can also put drawings up on a refrigerator, and I got the biggest one around. Think you can make a drawing for me to put up in the kitchen?" It had never occurred to him before, but suddenly he loved the idea of a collection of children's drawings up on the kitchen fridge. What made a kitchen more home than institution than drawings stuck up on the fridge?

Kent looked up at him, and the rare openness in the kid's eyes sunk right into Seb's chest. "You want this one?"

"I could have it?" The offer pleased him

deeply. "Really? Like I said, Franco's a pretty important guy around here."

"Sure."

Kids were like that, weren't they? Generosity came easy to them. Life hadn't taught them to judge or hoard—at least not much yet. Kids could also be mean, even at Charlie's and Kent's ages.

"Why's he important?" Kent scrunched up his eyebrows. "I mean, he's a fake frog."

"Well," Seb said, settling back against the tree for support when his muscles complained, "it's kind of Charlie and Mr. Mason and Ms. Dana's story to tell, but I think they'd be okay if I told you." He searched for the right starting point of the tender story. "You know Charlie's mom died, right?"

"In a car crash, yeah."

It still stung a bit how easily details of tragic accidents fell into conversations at the camp. It was part of the blessing—and the burden—of the place. "Yep. And Charlie's mom was from Hawaii, where they put flowers out on the water to remember people. Like we put flowers on graves here."

"We put flowers on Dad's grave. On holidays and his birthday and the day he got killed."

Seb wondered if a child saying a phrase like "got killed" would ever stop sounding like such a clash in his ears. "Charlie's mom would put out flowers for everyone who was gone on one special day." He pointed out to the pond that had finally returned to the west side of the property. For a terrible stretch, it had been a caked, dried mess of mud and cracked earth, but the drought that had seized the area had finally let up earlier this spring. There were a whole mess of people from North Springs Community Church who'd been praying that the pond would be back in time for Camp True North Springs to open, mostly on account of the story he was telling Kent right now. It was still much smaller than Mason said it had been in past years, but it was there, and that was a victory for sure.

"So every year on the special day, Mr. Mason and Charlie and his mom would put flowers out on the pond. For Charlie's grandma and two grandpas. And then for Charlie's mom, too." Seb reached out and stuck a finger in the steady stream of water that Franco spouted into his little pond. "Until last year when the pond dried up, and no one knew what to do. No one except Ms. Dana."

When Dana told the story, she always said

that God gave her the idea, that she would have never come up with it on her own. True or not, Seb didn't think now was the time to get into that theological detail with Kent.

Kent's gaze bounced between the natural pond in the distance and the decorative one in front of him. "I don't get it."

"She—well, she and a bunch of people from in town—gave this pond to Charlie so he'd have it on the day he needed one to put the flowers in. A stand-in until the big pond came back. So Charlie didn't have to miss his important day of remembering his mom and grandparents. Pretty neat, huh?"

Nothing short of a wondrous blessing, to hear Mason and Dana tell it. Charlie, too, for that matter. "Like I said, Franco's a big deal around here. I'd be proud to have a portrait of him on my fridge." There was something powerful in being able to refer to the enormous industrial fridge in the Camp True North Springs kitchen as *his* fridge.

While he'd never asked Mason and Dana, Seb felt it was okay to tell Kent the next part. "At the end of your stay here, you'll get a chance to send some flowers out on the big pond to remember your dad."

He watched Kent think about that for a moment, trying on the idea of the remembrance for size. "Okay." Then, after a bit of thought, he said, "We should get blue flowers. That was Dad's favorite color."

One point of guidance Dana and Mason had given all the camp staff was to always take a "tell me more" attitude when guests opened up about the loved ones they'd lost. This was the first time Seb would get to put that into practice, and he liked that it was with Kent. "Blue, huh? What kinds of things did your dad have that were blue?"

"Pajamas," Kent said with an echo of a smile. "He always wore blue pajamas. And Mom got him a blue bathrobe with his initials the Christmas before…" The smile disappeared as the words fell off.

Kent put the pad and pencil down. "He got shot, you know. By someone he didn't even know."

"I'm really sorry that happened." True as it was, it didn't feel like nearly enough. "And I expect everyone says that," Seb went on, "but it's true. It's wrong. I wish stuff like that didn't happen, especially to kids like you."

"Dad was a—" Seb watched Kent reach for the term "—bystander. He was driving home from the airport. It was late, and he went on a different road trying to get home quicker. There were guys there. They tried to steal Dad's car. And they shot him."

The facts seemed to pour out of the boy. "I woke up in the morning and there were all these people at my house—policemen and church people and my grandparents—and everyone was crying. Kimmy was still really little so she was awake with Mom, but I'd been asleep and the whole room stopped talking when I walked in."

Seb could see the remembered shock play across Kent's brown eyes. The boy gave a hard swallow and wrapped his arms around his skinny knees. "It was awful. I didn't want to go to sleep after that. I was scared what else would happen next time I woke up."

It wasn't even a conscious thought to wrap his arms around the small, sad boy. Seb just pulled him close and fought the wave of anger that surged up.

The steady, soothing stream of Franco's pond felt like the only thing holding the world in place as they sat there for a while, trying to make sense of something that would never make sense.

Chapter Four

Charlie explained an upcoming outing to Kate as they walked out of the art session. Tina Caldridge was still cutting paper dolls for Kimmy back in the barn and would bring her back to their guest room for a nap soon. "And so that's why we're going to the hardware store Saturday to build birdhouses," said the boy, with so much enthusiasm that it pinched Kate's heart. "I think Kent will have fun if he comes."

"I think he would, too, Charlie." In fact, they were looking for Kent to ask him to come. Kent hadn't been keen on joining in any of the activities. Kate was wondering how three weeks of this was going to turn out if her son didn't turn a corner soon. Kent was never the overly outgoing type, but he seemed to have lost what little joy he'd had since Cameron's death.

Charlie Avery was one of the reasons Kate had agreed to be one of the first families to visit the camp. But Charlie's presence was a double-edged sword. It showed Kate how someone so young could heal from something awful. But it also showed how far her own son had to go.

Charlie pointed toward the big house. "Look—there's Kent with Chef Seb over by Franco."

Kate glanced up to see the startling sight of Kent sitting curled up in a ball with Seb's arm around him. For a split second she thought she ought not to intrude—Kent kept his distance from so many people lately—but Charlie was already off and running toward the pair. By the time she caught up with the speedy eight-year-old, he'd already sat himself down on the other side of the little fountain. Kent had ducked out of Seb's hold the minute he'd seen his mom.

Seb retracted his arm as Kent moved, and Kate saw the telltale signs of Kent stifling tears. She caught Seb's eye as she drew closer. The man's expression told her what she'd already guessed—Seb's time with Kent around

Franco hadn't been a casual moment. How had that happened? Of all the people Kate expected Kent to connect with, the camp chef was last on her list.

"I just told Kent here about Franco," Seb said in a forced natural tone. "How important a frog he is around here and all."

"He's neat, isn't he?" said Charlie, just as brightly as before. "I was really sad about not having a pond to remember Mom and my grandparents by until Dana brought him to me."

Dana had mentioned something about a ceremony of some kind out by the pond— something about water and flowers—but what did this have to do with it?

Seb caught Kate's confused expression and gave a quick explanation of sending remembrance flowers out into the pond. It struck Kate as such a lovely and poignant thing that she felt her own throat tighten up.

"Hey, you drew him!" Charlie said, pointing at the sketch beside Kent. "Wow, that's good. You should definitely come with us to build the birdhouses on Saturday. Yours'll be awesome."

"Maybe," Kent said quietly.

Kate took that as a small victory. It wasn't

a "yes," but it wasn't the "No way!" she'd gotten about the outing yesterday.

"You want to go to the workshop and see the sample my dad has? I wanted to make my own the minute I saw it. We don't get to keep them—they go to the nature center—but I think that's even better." Charlie pulled on Kent's arm. "Come on."

Kent hesitated.

"Why don't you?" Kate said. "I'll keep your drawing safe until you get back." Kent had drawn something. That alone felt like a gigantic step forward.

"It's his," Kent said, pointing to Seb.

Nothing could have shocked Kate more. His first drawing in months and he gave it to Chef Seb? That seemed like too deep a connection too fast.

"I get to put it up on my fridge," Seb said, with such genuine pride it made Kate rethink her judgment. She had to admit, he seemed to recognize how big a thing the drawing was. That had to be worth something.

"Come on," Charlie urged. "I want you to see it."

Kate felt her heart squeeze in prayer the way it always did when she watched Kent wrestle with whether to take part in something—*anything*—lately. *Say yes, say yes*, her heart pleaded.

Kent got to his feet. "Okay."

Charlie took off toward the workshop just across the driveway, and Kent dragged himself up and after the boy. Not exactly enthusiasm, but she'd take it. She let out her held breath as the boys disappeared into the workshop doorway.

Seb shook his head as he labored to get himself off the ground and upright. "Kind of touch and go there for a moment," he admitted.

"What were you two talking about?" she asked, surprised she was a bit nervous to hear the answer.

Seb shifted his weight, bracing his hand on the lower part of his back. "Well, frogs and ponds at first." He turned to her. "And then he told me about the night his father died. About coming down in the morning to all the people in your house. The shock of it all, and how he was afraid to go to sleep and wake up to something worse."

Seb's whole face registered how much the story affected him. He pulled in a breath just as deep as the one she'd just let out. "I think one of the hardest things about working here is going to be hearing stories like that. I'm so sorry for his loss. For yours."

The stunned feeling must have shown on her face, because he added, "What? I didn't pry, honest."

Kate swallowed hard. "It's not that. He… he hasn't told that to anyone before."

Seb shook his head again and ran one hand across the back of his neck. "I had no idea."

He was one of those men who could pull off not taking much care with his looks—the rugged neglect only added to the charm. He needed a haircut, but it looked dashing rather than disheveled on him.

"I think it's good," Seb went on, squinting in the sunlight. "That he's opening up, I mean. I'm no counselor, but talking about it has to be good, right?"

Kate remembered the paralyzing shock of that morning. The kitchen filled with concerned friends and family, the exasperating effort to keep the chaos quiet so as not to wake Kent and Kimmy, the blackness of the night and the bleakness of the dawn. She felt as if she'd sleepwalked through the next few days, feeling numb and drowning in pain all at the same time. Talking about it was one of the only ways she could find cracks in that looming wall of grief. "It's worried me that he hasn't, actually. Seems too much for someone his age. I ask him questions, but..."

Seb offered a sad but sympathetic smile. "You're his mom. He's not supposed to like even ordinary questions from you. When I was his age, every tiny question from my mom felt like the Spanish Inquisition in cactus suits."

Kate laughed at the absurd visual. "You paint a vivid picture."

His tone softened. "How are you? It's been, what, a year?"

"About a year and a half." She shrugged. "Some days I feel like I'm finally coming out of it. It's still there—and sometimes it roars up at the oddest things—but you make a sort of peace with it. A widow friend said you get to the point where it walks alongside you rather than standing in front of you. That's about how it feels."

She looked at him. "Have you ever lost anyone?" She thought it was likely, given his working here.

"You heard me tell Kent about my grand-mother." He shifted again. "But the peaceful end of a happy life? That's not the same thing at all. I mean, I can't imagine..." He paused. "Is it okay to say that?"

Kate gave a sour laugh. "It's better than 'I know how you must feel.' I can't tell you how many times I heard that and wanted to shout, 'No, you don't!'"

"People say stupid things," he replied. "I think that's the whole point of camp. Everyone here gets it. No one's going to serve you up some trite saying or thoughtless remark."

She hugged her chest, feeling small but somehow safe. "Why are you here?" She'd been wondering what drew someone like Seb to a place like this.

He didn't answer at first. But he didn't leave, either, so Kate could only guess he was deciding how much to tell her. After a long pause of looking down at the sandy soil, he said, "I suppose my sponsor would tell you it's atonement."

She knew he'd used those particular words on purpose. The language of addiction. The force of it washed through her, a flurry of warning signs and worries. Kate couldn't work out quite what to say in response.

He read her response, recognizing that she knew those words and what they meant. "See? It's not just all of you who get a dose of the squigglies." He was trying to make light of it, but there was no making light of something like that.

Kate was ashamed how hard it was to meet his gaze. He didn't deserve the frightened judgment she knew must be showing up in her eyes. "So now you know. I keep waiting for it not to be so hard to tell someone, but I guess I'm not there yet."

He deserved the chance to explain his history. "How?"

"How did I become an addict?" Seb stretched and shifted again, both the subject and his body making him uncomfortable. "I want to say I'm not anymore. I'm clean. Haven't used for over a year." He pulled his recovery coin out of his pocket and rubbed it between his fingers. "Only, they tell you you're never not an addict. You're just in recovery. I can't think of a single thing I've ever done that was harder."

Seb watched her notice his choice of words. Addict, not alcoholic. Could he explain the downward spiral of drug abuse to someone like her? She was a physical therapist—she must understand the way pain could eat a soul alive. This story wouldn't increase her comfort, that was for sure.

Still, she was leery of Kent's connection to him, and clearly wanted to hear his story. She was turning herself inside out trying to find the sensitive way to ask. Here, of all places, she needn't have bothered. He didn't bother to swallow his laugh. "Don't ever play cards, Kate Hoyle. Your thoughts show up like neon on your face." He flipped the coin, caught it with the ease of the thousands of times he'd done it and slipped it back into his pocket.

"Painkillers. I'm thankful I escaped the really nasty stuff, but turns out there are plenty of other flavors out there to take a guy down. And plenty of shady characters ready to get you whatever you can pay for."

He watched her connect the dots. "The motorcycle accident."

He nodded. "At first it was merely to survive. Then…not so much. It was so easy to believe the lie that I could erase all the damage with a few pills. And I could—for a couple of hours. And then not so many hours. And then…" He flexed his fingers. It always felt as if it might take a fistfight to keep the memory at bay. "Well, I'll spare you the details. They call it 'rock bottom' for a reason."

"I'm sorry." There were those common heartfelt-yet-insufficient words. Someone ought to come up with better ones.

"Me, too," he groaned, arching his back slightly with a wince. "Every single day."

"You're still in a lot of pain." She didn't bother phrasing it as a question. "A few things are clear on your face, too," she added. Ah, so she could smile. He found himself wishing that pretty smile would show up more often. It was a sweet, light counterbalance to the weighty moment.

He was still in a lot of pain. Dreary daily pain that pulled on him every waking hour. "My brain—and Mason would say my soul—is firmly in recovery, but my back doesn't seem to have gotten the memo. It makes it so much harder. I know living with the pain is a way better choice than the pills, but some days… I doubt any of your fancy exercises would really help. It just *is*."

"What makes you so sure?" There was a defiance in her tone that pulled him off balance like an undertow. An optimism that he'd long since left behind, that didn't belong on someone who'd been through the tragedy she'd endured.

"Not everybody gets the happy ending." Even he was surprised by the sour tone of his words.

"But everyone can get better. Even a little bit better. I know some pain never goes away.

I work with chronic pain patients all the time. You can always find a little bit better. At least that's what I think."

"That's what you think, huh?" It wasn't fair how she kept saying things he found hard to resist. The tiny spark of hope she held out ran away with his resistance. It was as if his pain-filled life was Mason and Charlie's dried-up pond, and she, like Dana, offered a ceramic pond and a tin frog.

Did she realize it sounded like she was offering to work with him? Surely that was a really bad idea. Even if she did feel the same unwelcome pull he felt between them, it wasn't anything to mess with. Not in her fragile state or his messed-up one.

The truth was, Kate looked lonely. How could she not be? Loneliness could tell lies as strong as the ones told by his pills. You could draw up a list of all the possible benefits, and it still wouldn't match the risk of getting close to Kate or Kate getting close to him.

"Cameron's brother is an alcoholic." Kate blurted out the statement like a shield, which told him she'd been thinking the same things he'd been thinking. It was a bit of a blunt run for cover given the near offer she'd just made, but he could hardly blame her. Sensible people second-guessed getting involved with people like him. "He was doing great until Cameron died. That sent him back over the edge. I think he's back in meetings now, but I don't talk to him much."

Seb was quiet for a moment, allowing her the wise retreat. She was handing him reasons to stay away from her. Maybe from Kent and all of them. "So you've got some history there." He said it without any judgment, because, like his pain, it just was. Unalterable, irrevocable, like her husband's death.

"Too much," she answered quietly. "Cameron's dad, too. Never to the point that Gary got, but enough that Cameron never drank, ever." She stepped over and began picking out the leaves that had fallen into the fountain, as if she needed something to do with her hands. "It was a fight to even get Cameron to take cold medicine. He had so many bad memories that he lived on sort of nonstop alert, waiting for it to roar up inside him, I suppose." She swallowed. "For all the good it did."

"Are you angry? Still?" Only people who had scraped their way back up from the bottom had the right to ask a question like that.

The power of it made her turn to look at him. "Sometimes." He was grateful she'd chosen to be honest with him rather than give the polite answer. "I have friends with these shiny, happy lives. Honor roll kids and Sunday brunches and story hour at the library."

Seb gave a knowing shrug. "All that effortless happiness."

"Yes." She sighed. "I don't begrudge them that—mostly. But they take it all for granted." She stopped fussing with the fountain and leaned back against the tree. "I suppose I did once, too."

"I find myself wondering if all I get from here on in is an eighty percent life. *Good*, better than *fair*, but *excellent*'s off the table now." Seb shifted again, rolling one shoulder. "If I let myself think about it for too long, I start getting mad. It starts feeling unfair even though I've no one to blame but myself. And my body chemistry, depending on who you believe. I kid myself that I could handle the pain or the addiction, but handling both feels like a bit of a pile on." He was probably being too truthful with her, cutting too close to the bone, but he couldn't seem to stop himself. "That make any sense to you?"

"Yes, it does. As much as any of what's happened to us makes sense. And you're right—there are still too many days where 'widow' and 'single mother of young children' feel exactly like that—a pile on."

Seb studied her with a long look. She was so different from him. "I think you're hitting the high nineties—life percentage wise—if it's okay to say." He watched a heat rise to her cheeks that had nothing to do with the Arizona sunshine. It felt good to compliment her, and she deserved it. "Kent's a great kid and Kimmy is downright adorable. You'll make it through fine."

She laughed. More of a dark laugh than an amused one. "Oh, I've heard so many versions of those words since Cameron died. I want to believe them, you know? But I'm not so sure."

He ought to have pushed back against whatever was drawing him to her, but it was so easy to see the strength in her she couldn't see for herself. "I am."

"Why?"

"Don't know that I can say." He let himself hold her gaze for a moment before adding, "I just am."

He pulled himself away from the warmth of her company and headed back to the safety of his kitchen. Kate Hoyle was getting to him, and he wasn't sure at all what he ought to do about that.

Chapter Five

Thursday morning, Seb stood back to admire the sign Kent had drawn. "It's perfect. I wouldn't change a thing." The poster for the First-Ever Camp True North Springs Family Chili Cook-Off really was fabulous. And not just for a ten-year-old. Kent had drawn a big iron pot over a campfire, complete with a ladle boasting a bold blue first-place ribbon. He'd placed the day and time in little puffs of smoke coming off the fire, and some hungry-looking smiley faces in the background. The whole thing was cheerful and clever but not too fancy. Perfect. "Let's take it into the office to show Ms. Dana for her approval— but it's a shoo-in, if you ask me."

"Really?" Smiling Kent was a far cry from the grumpy kid who'd shown up in his kitchen mere days ago.

"Absolutely. Makes me want to enter, and I don't even qualify. If your dad's chili is as good as this poster, you've got no competition."

Kent pushed back from the dining room table where they'd been working. "Can we go show Mom first?" Seb was supposed to be working up menus for the coming week, but he had mostly ended up watching Kent draw. It was fun to see all the boy's intensity—and talent—focused on something positive.

"Sure thing."

The cook-off was actually a complicated hassle. Coordinating kitchen times, finding enough utensils for four different sets of cooks and getting ingredients for each family's recipe was turning into a massive undertaking. Not to mention the "security"— making sure each family's recipe and tactics were kept secret from the others. Why hadn't he come up with something more cooperative than a cook-off?

"Where are Mom and Kimmy, anyway?"

That question was a minor victory in itself. For the first days of camp, Kent had stuck close to his mom and sister when he wasn't sulking in the guest room. He'd insisted on knowing where they were if he wasn't with them.

Dana and Mason had noticed, too. They'd both worked on the boy's comfort level, and Kent had slowly let his constant guard down. The whole staff took it as a victory that Kent was coming to trust that Kate and Kimmy would be safe even if he wasn't nearby.

"What's better than watching the freedom of childhood slowly find its way back into some kid's life?" Dana had remarked. Everyone agreed.

Trouble was, most of Kent's "Where's Kate?" radar had somehow transferred itself to Seb. He found himself wondering where Kate was, what she was doing, how her days were going. Was she easing up like Kent? Was the camp beginning to give her the respite she was seeking?

Even when he was busy in the kitchen during meals, he felt her presence in the dining room nearby. He cooked for everybody, but some small part of him cooked especially for Kate. For Kimmy and her specific needs, yes, but also for Kate. The desire to make her happy, to lighten her life, to make her smile, had surged up in him in ways that ought to worry him. After all, it had only been a handful of days and already the intensity of his awareness of her seemed to be getting out of hand.

She was a guest. He was staff. There were certain lines you didn't cross, right?

"Oh, I remember now," Kent said, pulling Seb from his rebellious thoughts. "They're in the garden. Come on!"

It was no small feat to make things grow in the Arizona climate, but Mason and Dana had created a little garden and greenhouse as part of the camp property. Raised beds, shade and a regular watering schedule meant Seb actually had a selection of fresh herbs to harvest and the promise of vegetables like tomatoes and zucchini by the end of the summer if it wasn't too scorching.

But as Mason reminded him, it was mostly for the families. Some folks from the North Springs Garden Club had convinced him of the healing properties of nature and growing things. Seb had to agree. Sometimes it was hot, sweaty work that he was glad mostly fell in the groundskeeper's job description, but other times it really was a good way to calm a chaotic mind.

Kate was in the back corner, under an awning that shaded a little patch of optimistic tomato vines. She had her hands deep in the earth, looking more settled than he'd seen her earlier in the week.

So it was working. Camp True North Springs was doing what it was supposed to do—giving these families a chance to restore and reset. He watched her for a moment, intent and smiling, talking in happy tones to Kimmy, who sat next to her with a toy shovel and pail.

She was beautiful. The thought landed on him with power and without warning. Not pretty—he'd met loads of women who fit that description, but it never went below the surface—but a sort of beautiful that didn't come from makeup or a hairstyle. In fact, her hair was messy, she didn't have a speck of makeup on and there was a big smudge of mud on one cheek. And yet he found her breathtakingly beautiful. It drew him like a campfire on a cold night. It lodged somewhere in him, deep and stubborn. Seb couldn't remember having that reaction to any woman, much less one who was as off-limits as Kate.

You are in way over your head here. Be careful. Be realistic. Hang on for a few more weeks and she'll be gone.

That was a joke. Even as his brain tried to make the argument, Seb knew it would be a long time before he forgot Kate and her children.

Fortunately, Kent barreled into the garden ahead of him, holding up the sign. "Mom, look what Chef Seb and I made!"

Seb didn't even realize how much he'd been waiting for Kate's smile until her face broke wide open in a beam of delight.

"Oh, honey, it's wonderful!" she praised as she pulled off her garden gloves and carefully examined the poster Kent brought to her. She'd been so worried about Kent's refusal to draw. It was half the reason he'd asked Kent to make the posters in the first place—they weren't really needed. He just wanted Kent to have the chance to make them.

"It's all Kent," Seb corrected as he caught up to them. It really was like coming up to a campfire. The glow off Kate was nearly a physical sensation. "Kid's got talent." He risked the pain he knew would come from squatting down beside the family, just because it felt so nice to be close to them.

"Dirt!" Kimmy said, raising a shovelful of sandy soil up to him for inspection. "I'm helping."

"She may actually agree to eat a carrot after this," Kate said with a laugh.

Seb grinned at Kimmy. "Did you know I

can make a palm tree out of a carrot and a green pepper?"

Kimmy scrunched up her face in doubt. Kate raised an eyebrow at the boast. "You don't strike me as the garnish type."

"More for amusement than any fancy stuff. I got a lot of kids to feed. Sometimes I figure it's gonna take a trick or two. Or twelve." It was then that his back chose to remind him why he rarely squatted down these days. Seb took a second to try to figure out how to get back up without looking like a ninety-year-old and failed miserably.

Kate thrust the little shovel she'd been holding into the dirt like a soldier planting a flagpole. "That's it. We're going over there." She pointed to a small patch of grass outside the garden fence.

Seb tried to protest, but Kate had her "do as you're told" mom face on now. Or maybe her therapist face. Neither one meant Seb was going back to check on the chicken thawing for lunch anytime soon. He tried to mind and failed miserably at that, too.

Kent knew his mom meant business. "You'd better go."

Kate stood up, hands on her hips, while Seb sheepishly grabbed on to the garden fence to support his body while he made his way to standing. Man, it hurt. He'd been skipping the exercises the last therapist had foisted on him months ago, and now he was paying dearly for it. Probably about to pay more.

"Did someone give you exercises for that back? Ones that you actually do?" Kate asked in a tone that let Seb know she already knew the answer. Where did moms learn to read minds like that?

"I have a folder somewhere," he admitted, only because that sounded slightly better than "No."

After eyeing the patch of grass for a moment, Kate commanded, "Lie down. Faceup."

It felt ridiculous. Less so, however, when Kent and even Kimmy did so right beside him. Seb was grateful for their companionship on whatever journey of pain Kate was about to lead him on.

"How do you get out of bed in the morning?"

The ordinary question felt loaded given how much he'd been trying to tamp down his attraction to the woman currently looming over his shoulder. "Reluctantly?"

Kent laughed.

"There's a right way and a wrong way. My guess is you've been doing the wrong way."

"And I expect I'm about to learn the right way," Seb replied. He squinted up at Kate, who had clearly shifted into professional mode. That was good. It made it slightly easier having her address him as a patient. But only slightly.

"Deep breath, please. In and out, from the core."

"Huh?" Everyone always talked to him about breathing from his core, but the way he figured it, that was about a foot lower than where his lungs were. How on earth were you supposed to breathe from below your lungs?

Kate somehow heard his resistance. "Let's try this. Lie still and press your lower back into the grass."

Easy enough. Rather nice, actually. Lying down always seemed to take a load off his back. He closed his eyes, and just for fun made a snoring noise.

Kimmy giggled. Even Kent made a small snicker from his other side.

Kate was not amused. "Kimmy, find Chef Seb's belly button. Gently."

Seb opened one eye to watch Kimmy scramble upright. She then planted her hands hard enough on Seb's midsection that he gave a little *umph*. This wasn't like anything any of those gruff old therapists had done back at the hospital.

"Engage those muscles under Kimmy's hands and tell me about your injury. I want you to engage and breathe at the same time."

He followed her directions, feeling the grass under him and Kimmy's wiggly fingers on top of him while he told her which bones and muscles had been injured in the bike crash. It was weird. But also fun. And nothing hurt…yet.

He watched Kate take a moment to analyze what he'd told her, one finger pressed in thought to the memorable rose of her lips. "Okay, you're going to want to always get out of bed on your left side. You can take your hands away, Kimmy. Seb, I want you to roll toward Kent. Go slow, and don't get up. Just get on your side."

Seb rolled to his side as directed. He shot Kent a funny face as he did so, and Kent returned the favor with a goofy grin of his own as they lay face-to-face on the grass.

"She does this to everybody," the boy whispered.

Seb couldn't decide if that was a good

thing. An irrational part of him wanted special treatment from Kate.

"Top hand on the ground in front of you," Kate directed. Kent demonstrated, and Seb followed suit.

"Now, don't use your back to get up, push yourself upright with your arm until you can swing your legs around. This will be easier on a bed, of course, but you get the idea."

Kent popped up like a prairie dog. It took Seb a bit longer. But he had to admit, it didn't produce the zing of pain he usually felt getting out of bed in the morning. "Well, what do you know? It works."

"Using your muscles the proper way always makes a big difference." She was trying to hide the "I told you so" that played all over her face.

Seb liked how easily he could read her. It made him feel as if the connection he felt with her wasn't all in his imagination. "Just getting out of bed, huh? That'll fix everything?" He fought the uncharacteristic urge to wink.

"Well, no." A blush rose in her cheeks. "But like I said, it should make a big difference."

Seb pulled his feet underneath him to sit cross-legged on the grass, planted like a row of vegetables between Kimmy and Kent. "I might just have to start listening to you now." Kimmy giggled, Kent moaned and Seb liked the way both sounds landed in his ears.

His affection for this family was running the risk of getting out of hand. He ought to be worried about that, but he just couldn't bring himself to be.

"It's not so bad."

Not exactly a rave review, but Kate was pleased at Kent's response when she asked him what he thought of his first week at camp Friday morning. Kimmy was still sleeping, and they were whispering in their pajamas— something they used to do way back before their world fell apart. Kent was looking down at her from the top bunk, his hair mussed from sleep but his eyes wide, a welcome echo of the boy she missed so much. The smile was still rare, but it showed up more than it used to. She'd even caught him drawing several times, sketching up ideas for the birdhouses they'd be making on their first "field trip" into town over the weekend.

The smell of breakfast wafted in through the window. "The food's good, isn't it?" The food had been wonderful. And to not have to be the one to buy it, cook it, clean up after it? Well, that was downright wonderful. She told herself that's why she was enjoying the meals at camp so much. Not the handsome man who made them.

Kent eyed her. "You don't freak out when we eat anymore."

"You're right," she admitted. Slowly, over the course of the last week, her near-constant red alert at eating with other people had eased up. Part of it was that now those dangerous, sure-to-misunderstand strangers were becoming friends. Friends who understood and respected the challenge of keeping Kimmy safe from her allergies.

Another part of it was the constant reassurance Seb gave her that he was watching out for Kimmy. She'd been on guard by herself for so long. It touched her deeply that she had a partner of sorts—even if it was a staff person and only for a few weeks.

Kent flopped on his back, drawing imaginary circles on the guest room ceiling with his fingers. "Will she grow out of it, you think? Will she be like this forever?"

Such an enormous question for such a small girl. "We don't really know. Some things get better for some kids as they get older. Some don't. We just test things very carefully when Dr. Hutchens says it's time, and hope."

"It's not fair."

Kate couldn't argue with that. "No, it's not. None of it's been fair."

"How come we had all this bad stuff happen to us? I mean, Lewis hasn't had a bad thing happen to him his whole life. They go on great vacations every year and all of his grandparents are still alive. How come?"

Kate stood up and leaned on the bunk so that her face was close to his. "I ask myself that all the time. And I ask God when I get sad and mad. It's kind of like Kimmy's allergies—nobody really knows."

Kent didn't care much for that answer. "Well, that rots."

She had to laugh at that. "It sort of does. But I do know that even the people who look like they have perfect lives don't. They just have hurts and problems that don't show on the outside as much as ours. And I know plenty of people who have had a load of bad things happen to them and still manage to end up happy. It's just sort of a dented, in-spite-of kind of happy. Like Chef Seb's back."

Kent rolled back over to look at her. "What do you mean?"

"Well, you know Chef Seb's back hurts him. A lot. But he still finds a way to cook, and he seems like he has fun. It'd be like missing Dad's supersecret chili ingredient, but still finding a way to make a pretty good batch, anyway." Not the most brilliant metaphor in the world, but she hoped it got the point across.

"We're gonna have all the ingredients for Dad's chili. Chef Seb promised. He says he's sure I'm gonna win."

Not exactly a wise promise to make to a boy. Especially one who'd had as many hard knocks as Kent. "Chef Seb seems awfully sure of himself. Don't you think you could have fun even if you don't win?"

"No."

Kate sighed. She was going to have to work on how much focus Seb was giving this contest. It was great that Kent was engaged and excited, but the last thing she needed was anyone setting her son up for disappointment.

Chapter Six

There were probably a dozen reasons why he shouldn't be doing this, why he should be seeing to this baking on his own, but Seb couldn't think of any of them this morning.

I'm inviting more families next week, he told himself. *Every family will get a chance to help make the cookies for church coffee hour.* This was about inventive participation, not wrangling more time with the Hoyle family. At least that's how he would explain it to Mason if he asked. Mason had, in fact, given him a gently worded warning about the special treatment he was giving the Hoyle family.

Seb had promised to have a baking session with all the families so as not to show any favoritism. "In the Kitchen with Seb" was a good programming idea, and a creative way to keep building bridges between the camp and the community down the mountain in North Springs. People were coming around, but not everyone was on board with Mason and Dana's mission.

Kimmy burst through the kitchen doors first—ahead of Mom for a welcome change—and handed Seb a boldly colored finger-painted masterpiece. "For the fridge!" she pronounced.

"Wow!" Seb gushed with ease. It pleased him to no end that his kitchen would be filled with children's artwork. It was such a warm touch of home—and one he couldn't remember at all from his own strained childhood. *Warm* and *colorful* weren't ever words he'd use to describe how he grew up. Maybe that's why food had become such an important part of his life—it was a way to get some of that back. And now to give some of that back to the church and the people of North Springs.

Kate still looked nervous. "Are you sure this is a good idea?" Kate still seemed to view the kitchen as a minefield of threats to Kimmy.

"I am. I want this little chef here to know food can be fun." He produced a pint-size apron and goofy mini chef's hat he'd found at a kitchen store down in town.

"It's pink!" Kimmy squealed, clapping her hands.

Kate tried unsuccessfully to scowl. "That's cheating." The forced frown never reached the delight in her blue eyes.

Seb produced a red-striped apron for Kate and handed one of his own denim ones to Kent. "Not if you have one for everybody." Kent gave a small eye roll, but tied his on. *Good. We've got everyone on board for this.*

He tied his own apron on and clapped his hands together. "Now, let's go over our Kimmy rules again, just to be safe."

Seb was looking to Kate, but Kimmy piped up instead. "No nuts," she declared, counting off on tiny fingers. "No cows. No fishies."

"Why didn't I think of putting it that way?" Seb asked. It sounded much more fun than no dairy, no nuts and no shellfish. After giving Kate an impressed look over the self-advocating skills of her daughter, Seb hoisted Kimmy up on a stepladder with a rim around the outside. Kent didn't need a stool of any kind, but the contraption placed her safely at counter height, which was exactly his plan. "And good thing you can have egg substitutes, because that gives us lots of cookies we can make. Now, we know you like strawberries."

"Yep!" Kimmy's pigtails bobbed with her enthusiastic nod.

"So today we're going to make strawberry thumbprint cookies. No nuts, no cows and certainly no fishies."

"Got it," Kimmy agreed.

"Where did you find a recipe?" Kate asked.

"A good chef never reveals his secret recipes, right, Kent?"

Kent, still seeming to find the whole thing a bit uninteresting, at least gave a nod. "Sure."

"Okay, let's get started. We've got a lot of cookies to make. Then I'll bring them down tomorrow morning to Mrs. Salinas in town while you all are having your outing. She's really nice—you'll meet her," he said to Kimmy and Kate. "She's in charge of setting them out at church."

"We have a cookie lady at our church," Kent said. "She's old."

Kate looked horrified. "But she makes *delicious* cookies," she offered in amendment to Kent's lack of tact.

"Mrs. S runs the bed-and-breakfast in town, so she's a great cook, too." He gave Kent a good-natured glare. "You're about to find out it's about talent, not age. And team-work. We have some real talent in the kitchen this morning, so let's get this team to work."

With that, Seb tightened the knot on his apron, pointed to the collection of ingredients on the counter behind them and began issuing instructions. Kate hadn't felt anything but anxiety in a kitchen for a long time, but Seb was clearly out to change that. Talent or no talent, allergies notwithstanding, the Hoyles were going to bake this morning—and have fun doing it.

An hour later, Kate tried to look around the kitchen without a sense of shock. The mess would give any mother pause. She, Kimmy, Kent and Seb were getting outrageously messy in this impromptu cookie-baking session.

Kate was tidier about her exploits in the kitchen, but Seb went after it with abandon. All three of them—and most anything nearby— were covered in flour and sticky strawberry filling.

"I forgot how much fun this is," Kate admitted. She should have been horrified at the state of Seb's kitchen, but seeing how Seb wasn't, it coaxed her into not caring as much.

She'd been here a matter of days, but what a difference that time had made. Each day she seemed to shed a new layer of weight. To be honest, Kate worried that whatever was all the way underneath those layers would be raw and tender. Still, hadn't working in the garden taught her that's how new growth was supposed to be?

Seb's easy talent for having fun with the kids was a big part of it. He was making a big deal out of Kimmy's participation in the current batch of strawberry jam thumbprint cookies.

"Has anyone ever told you how *excellent* your thumb is for cookie making?" He held Kimmy's hand as if she were Princess of Everything. Kate told herself it was absurd—and unwise—to be envious. *I feel like my pain takes away all my joy. How does Seb have so much despite his pain? He seems to be a different man around me and Kimmy and Kent.* She tried to tell herself she was imagining the difference.

"I beat Kent twice," Kimmy said, raising both her thumbs.

When Seb's eyebrows furrowed, Kate offered an explanation. "Cameron used to thumb wrestle with Kent."

Seb looked shocked. "You wrestle with these thumbs? These excellent thumbs?" he teased Kimmy.

"Mommy, show him how," Kimmy said.

Kate's pulse jumped. "I'm sure Chef Seb knows how to thumb wrestle." Suddenly the charming little game felt silly.

Seb's expression was downright rascally as he shook his head. "Nope. But now I gotta try it, right?"

She was cornered. Either she was going to have to admit to being afraid to touch Seb's hands or she was going to have to talk her way out of this. The mischief in Seb's eyes told her the latter wouldn't work.

"Mommy will win," Kimmy warned Seb, in a singsong voice.

"That's what you think," Seb countered. "I learn fast. And I don't let girls win just because they're girls." He pulled up a chair opposite Kimmy and Kate. "Show me how."

He already knew how. She knew that, and Seb had to know she knew that. This was far closer to flirting than it was to recreation or any kind of culinary art. That should be bad—it certainly was scary—but there was something else pulling at her just as hard. There was such a long-forgotten warmth about Seb's attentions. To have someone look at her the way Seb did, with no history and not the ever-present pity and concern that seemed to surround her back in Pennsylvania. It made the raw, tender spots feel fresh and new, foolish as it seemed.

She placed her hand on the counter, which was still covered in flour and puddles of strawberry filling. Kate cupped her fingers and raised her thumb, ignoring how her breath caught as she nodded to Seb to do the same. For all the game Kimmy thought it was, it felt more like holding hands.

He slid his hand next to hers, fitting his cupped fingers against hers. She tightened against his grip, and he against hers. It felt absurd to notice how perfectly their hands fit together, how warm and solid his hand felt around hers. It took an enormous amount of effort to sound casual. "So without loosening our grip—" the "our" seemed to stick out like their thumbs "—we try to pin each other's thumb down."

Seb adjusted his hand to hold hers more tightly, and Kate felt the slight friction caused by the flour still on both their fingers. "On three," she said, hoping against hope that at some point this would feel more like play and less like…well, holding hands with a very handsome man who had just given her daughter a tremendous gift.

Seb narrowed one eye. "Sounds silly."

Kimmy planted her hands on her tiny hips, a bit of her mother's bossiness shining through the overload of cuteness. "It *is* silly."

"But unlikely to injure your back. Or anything else. Except maybe your pride," Kate boasted. "When I beat you. After all, I am a *girl*." She brandished that last word like the challenge it was. Where had that come from?

Seb adjusted his position as if he were ready to give her the battle of her thumb-wrestling career. For all the risk of touching him, of the gentle but insistent grip he had on her hand at the moment, it felt…fun. Fun had been missing from her life for so, so long. "On three," she explained, turning to Kimmy. "Will you count for us?"

Kimmy looked thrilled. She held up a trio of fingers with great importance. "One… two…three!"

The next minute was filled with wagging thumbs, wild cries, chaotic effort and no small amount of flour flying about the room. It would have been wiser to clean up the powder before launching into the match, but somehow it just added to the fun of it all. "Ha!" Kate cried out as she pinned Seb's thumb. "Gotcha!"

Kimmy clapped, sending a small white cloud puffing up around her palms. "Mommy won!"

"Mommy won *this round*," Seb corrected, not letting go of Kate's hand even when she tried to pull it away.

His expression left Kate wondering if she truly had bested him or he'd just let her *think* she'd done so. "I don't let girls win just because they're girls," he'd said. She wasn't so sure she believed him. Seb resettled himself against the counter with serious intent. "Two out of three."

She shouldn't, but she did.

Seb pinned her thumb in half the time it had taken her to pin his. "Like I said, I learn fast," he declared. "And I don't let girls win *just because*."

Kate had trouble believing the chef had made it to his age—Seb seemed to be in his early thirties, just as she was—without knowing what thumb wrestling was. Nor could she be certain she'd won fair and square. What was certain, however, was that the winner of the next round would take the match. And also, if she were honest, how much she was enjoying this silly game and the attentions of her handsome opponent. He'd not let go of her hand yet. And whether she was willing to admit it or not, she enjoyed the contact.

After Kimmy's gleeful count, and no small flurry of flour, Seb pinned Kate's thumb with something close to ease. And when he ended the match, he held her hand for a treacherous moment longer than necessary before releasing it.

She felt the absence of his clasp immediately. The sensation had nothing to do with the lost match and all too much to do with the look in Seb's eyes.

"I like a worthy opponent," he said, one corner of his mouth turning up in a very charming grin.

Kate was trying to think of something— anything—safe to say to that when the oven timer went off. *Saved by the bell indeed.* Seb wheeled around to slide the two enormous cookie sheets from the oven and show off what they'd baked.

"Who knew what all these thumbs could do?" he said, wiggling his own until Kimmy giggled and joined in. He caught Kate's eye before adding, "We make a pretty good team, don't we?"

"Yep!" declared Kimmy, giving an enthusiastic thumbs-up.

We do, Kate thought in the privacy of her heart. *And I don't know what to do about that.*

Chapter Seven

Rita Salinas gave Seb a wide smile as she accepted the containers of cookies. "You were busy this morning!"

"I had a little help. I've decided to have each of the families help me bake the church cookies. Their participation might make it easier to come to church, and it might sway a few of the townsfolk in our favor."

"I've always said good baking can smooth out a lot of rough edges."

"Actually," Seb said, "I need a bit of advice, too. Baking advice." He told her the story of promising Kate Hoyle a lemon meringue pie with no actual skills to back it up. "It doesn't look like the kind of thing you can just whip up following a video. There are a lot of 'pie fail' shots on social media, and I can't afford to fail this one."

Rita saw through his very practical explanation in a heartbeat, resulting in a "you should know better" look Mason would have enjoyed. "You actually told her lemon meringue pie was a specialty of yours when you had no idea how to make one." After a moment, the scowl left her face and she winked. "Just how pretty is she?"

Seb wasn't quite sure how to safely answer that question. He settled for, "Doesn't matter. She's a camp mom. *Very* off-limits. I'm just trying to do my job well. There seems to be an art to the meringue part, and I know you make them."

"True," Rita said. "You can make a delicious crust and filling, but if the meringue fails, it's all gone." The older Latina woman eyed him. "Took me a few years to master."

"Yeah, well, they've already been here a week. I better serve up a great pie soon, or she'll know."

Rita pulled out one of her cookbooks. "She knows already. A woman can spot that kind of *engaño* a mile off." Her narrowed eyes left no need for translation. "How much time do you have?"

"Now?" He wasn't counting on tackling this now, seeing how Friday was spaghetti night at camp, but he might just have enough time to pull this off.

"You want to make an appointment for next week?" she teased.

When he didn't answer, Rita flipped open the cookbook and pointed to a set of aprons hanging on the wall. "Grab one, wash up and get out the eggs. We're making pie."

As he followed her directions, Seb offered something else he'd come to say. "Thank you. And not just for this. We both know I wouldn't have this job without you and Bart supporting the camp."

Rita gave him one of her warm smiles as she began separating the eggs—whites into one bowl and yolks into another. "Nobody needs to thank me for keeping Arthur Nicholson from getting his way on that one. You tell Dana and Mason to be careful. He's just waiting for something to go wrong up there. Reach that cornstarch off the top shelf for me, will you?"

Seb reached carefully for the yellow box, glad to feel his back cooperating a bit more today. Turns out getting out of bed correctly *did* make a difference. "I think Mason and Dana know." Everybody up on the mountain knew Arthur Nicholson was just waiting for this test session to fail in some way. Camp True North Springs was so much more than what Nicholson cast it to be.

Rita's smile widened. "And he popped the question. I'm so happy for those two. Bart and I are going to do everything we can to help them. Which I guess includes—" she laughed again as she accepted the box from Seb "—helping a certain cook make good on a very shaky promise of pie."

Seb leaned down and gave Rita a peck on the cheek. "You're a lifesaver, Rita."

She batted him away with a good-natured swat that he could feel left a white smudge on his chin. "And you're too much of a charmer, Chef. Now, we let those egg whites warm up while we cook the crust and start on the filling."

Just an hour later, armed with Rita's many tips for success, Seb slid a remarkably good-looking pie from the oven. "Will you look at that?" he crowed—until the fluffy white meringue began to slide disobediently off the yellow custard filling. Seb yelped and tilted the pie to keep from losing the top completely. Still, it now looked more mudslide than masterpiece.

Rita's gaze bounced from his frown to the

lopsided dessert. "Not bad for a first effort. We didn't get the custard hot enough before we put the meringue on—that's what makes it weep."

Seb moaned. "I'm gonna be weeping if I don't nail this on the second try." He could not serve this pie and claim it was a specialty. Certainly not to Kate.

"It probably tastes just fine," Rita consoled. "And here's an idea for you—you could always just tell her the truth."

Seb was opening his mouth to refute that plan when he heard Bart, Rita's husband, coming down the hallway. "What are you cooking up now, *carina*?" Bart gave a dubious look at the white peaks of the uneven meringue slope. "Looks like your pie had a bit of a mishap," he said to his wife. "Does that mean we get to eat all of it rather than the guests?" He clearly found this a happy accident.

"It's my mishap," Seb admitted sourly. "She was teaching me and I failed."

"You did not fail," Rita corrected with a motherly tone. "You just didn't reach perfection. That's not the same thing."

"My wife speaks the truth. And her less than perfection is almost always still delicious." Bart looked ready to sample the pie right now, even though it hadn't even begun to cool. "Is this a pie recipe for the camp?"

"It's a pie for a camper," Rita said with a look Seb regretted instantly. "A favorite of one of the moms." Seb waited for Rita to out his ill-fated claim to the pie being a specialty of his, but at least she left that part out. He tried again to tilt the meringue layer back into its proper position, but it just slid around like a fluffy iceberg in a lemon sea.

Rita jutted her chin out. "It didn't take, honey. Nothing for it this time." When Seb felt his lower lip stick out in a pout that would do Kent proud, she swatted his shoulder. "You know the altitude can make baking tricky up here."

Seb stared at the pie. "You can keep this one if you like."

"You mean I can *eat* this one if I like," Bart revised. Just as his wife was opening her mouth, he added, "Not until it cools, yes, I know." He nodded to the container of cookies sitting on the far counter. "Church cookies? I can't think of a better way to beat Arthur Nicholson at his own game than the camp providing the church cookies."

"It's better than that. The camp families are

doing the baking," Rita explained. "I'd like to see Arthur try and bad-mouth those families while eating their cookies."

Nicholson had given more than one speech about the dangers of "those kinds of families" spending time in quaint North Springs. As if the town had no faults or problems of its own. Seb was rather proud of the speech he'd given right back to Nicholson at a town meeting. It was the first time he'd clearly declared how the rehab center just outside town had brought him to North Springs. The first time he'd openly spoken of his addiction.

It had been a moment of victory of sorts for him. People in town behaved as he'd hoped—they welcomed him and his support of the camp. Nicholson, on the other hand, had never looked at him the same way again. The whole "damaged goods" glare Seb could spot a mile away these days.

"Are you coming into town with them tomorrow?" Bart asked.

"No. They gave me the morning off." Seb untied the apron and hung it back up with the others. "I might be in town taking care of a few errands, but it'll be Dana and Mason who will be leading the families around."

"I'm so happy the girls are coming here for

tea and cupcakes. I can't wait to meet them. And I know Mike at the hardware store is pleased as punch to be getting the boys to make birdhouses for the nature center. It's going to be a great day. I hope Arthur sees every minute of it."

You and me both, Seb thought as he bid goodbye to his sorry excuse for a pie. *We all need a win here.*

Saturday morning arrived, the day for the official camp outing to North Springs. Kate had noticed the community's beauty as they'd driven through it on the way to the camp. Now she was looking forward to an afternoon wandering the shops that were arranged around the town square.

Kate found it a charming town, the kind of place where anyone would want to live. It was like a picture postcard, with a green space surrounding a center town hall–like building. A lovely gazebo sat on one side of the lawn, while benches and little paths wound around the other sides. A billboard with notices for friendly sounding events like potlucks and pancake breakfasts made the place sound idyllic.

All sorts of shops—the kind of thing she

loved and the kind of thing Kent had no patience for—called to her and Kimmy for a perfectly girly afternoon. The whole thing would start off with lunch and cupcakes at the Gingham Pocket Bed-and-Breakfast. Rita Salinas, true to Seb's promise, had proven very cooperative about food safety for Kimmy when Kate had called ahead. It was shaping up to be a treasure of a day, really.

Some camp families drove their own cars, while others hitched a ride on a small yellow bus driven by the Busketeers. Evidently North Springs boasted its own corps of volunteer school bus drivers, headed up by Rita's husband, Bart. While that sounded fun, Kate opted for her car with the right car seat for Kimmy. And if Kimmy didn't last the afternoon and needed a nap, she'd be able to head back without inconveniencing the other families.

Dana and Mason called them all into a group next to the gazebo. "Okay, then," Mason said, clapping his hands to get attention. "Boys, you head off with me to Guerro's Diner for tacos before we meet up with Mike at the hardware store." He pointed out the diner and store, both visible from where they were standing.

"Girls," Dana continued, "you come with me for lunch and a craft over at the Gingham Pocket with Rita." She pointed to a lovely house behind her with a wide porch and window boxes overflowing with colorful flowers.

Tina Caldridge raised her hand.

"Yes?" Mason said.

"What if some girls would rather do tacos and birdhouses than crafts and tea sandwiches?"

Kate had wondered the same thing, actually. The activities did seem rather stereotypically divided between male and female.

Dana stepped up. "You absolutely can, Tina. And if any of the guys would rather go to the Gingham Pocket, that's fine, too."

The boys looked at each other, more than a bit curious as to who would do such a thing. For a moment, Kate wondered if Kent would opt for the safety of being with her and Kimmy—they were painting flowerpots for the church garden, after all. She'd been thrilled to see Kent spending time with Charlie, and wanted them to have this afternoon together to deepen that new friendship.

Tina let out a laugh. "I'm going with the girls. But you should think about letting us choose next time."

"Good point," Mason said. Kate liked how he'd taken any suggestion from this trial group of families seriously. He really was intent on making this the best experience possible for his guests.

Kate's shoulders relaxed as Kent waved. "See ya later, Mom. Have fun, Kimmy."

"You, too!" Kimmy called to her brother.

"I hope they know what's coming." Heidi Boswell shook her head as her two sons followed Mason and the rest of them. "Those boys eat like five instead of two, and I don't think they know how to use a hammer. I pity the birds who get to live in their houses."

"Mason's an excellent teacher," Dana said. The woman's eyes lit up every time she talked about her new fiancé, and Kate felt her heart pinch just a bit. "And they can use glue if Mike thinks any thumbs are in danger of getting smashed."

Any mention of thumbs cast Kate's mind back to the antics in the kitchen yesterday and made her heart pinch a bit more. She was glad to have an afternoon away from the camp and the pull of Seb's attentions. She needed time to sort out her surprising new feelings.

They had a few minutes to walk up and down the block before heading into lunch. As they did, Kate noticed things. The sidewalks were crowded with weekend shoppers. One or two people eyed the Boswell and Domano families, labeling them as city people without any facts whatsoever. Looking across the square, Kate watched a woman make no attempt to hide her wariness at the size of the Domano brothers as they headed toward the hardware store. Those boys had sweet dispositions. The assumptions happening around her struck her as deeply unfair. A reminder of all the reasons the camp had been such a refreshing break from the real world.

They would have to go back to the real world soon enough. *Can today just be a lovely day? A pretty memory?* Kate found herself sending up a prayer as she and Kimmy walked into the Gingham Pocket. *Let today be perfect*, she pleaded. *Just one pretty, perfect day to remind me there can be others.* Her heart was beginning to think that all the nice things could only happen inside Camp True North Springs, and that sort of thinking would never come to good.

Chapter Eight

Seb pulled in a deep breath of clear mountain air. A few hours off with no meal to cook felt like a luxury.

After feeding four families three meals a day for five days, Seb was grateful for the free time. Running the camp kitchen was harder than he'd anticipated. Not the cooking part—he'd had enough restaurant experience to handle that—but the emotional toll of wanting to meet everyone's individual needs. The desire to make each camper's experience as healing as possible. While his extroverted personality liked the constant hum of people around camp, even that had its limits. So he was grateful that everyone—staff and campers—was down in town on their excursion.

He'd spent the first hour basking in the solitude of having the whole property to himself. After that, he drove downtown to take care of a few things and do what every chef enjoyed: eating someone else's great cooking.

He ducked into Guerro's Diner—a favorite of both Mason's and his—being sure to time his arrival after the herd of Camp True North Springs boys would have made their way to the hardware store to begin building the birdhouses for the nature center. In truth, part of him wanted to join them. He was curious as to how Kent—with all his artistic talents—would tackle the job.

But given the way his thoughts were tangled up in that family lately, Seb decided some distance was a better choice. He'd spent that solo hour up at the camp sorting through his thoughts, trying to figure out what to do with the urge to stay close to the Hoyle family. It was becoming an issue.

Who am I kidding? It's already an issue. Seb just didn't know what to do about it.

As he turned the corner to the street just off the square where Guerro's was, his hand tingled with the memory of Kate's fingers against his. Thumb wrestling was a silly game, but he'd gladly agreed not only for Kimmy's sake, but for the chance to feel

Kate's touch. They both denied it, but they both knew it to be true.

"Well, look who I see." A vaguely familiar voice came from behind him.

He turned, and felt his body go stiff at the sight. Vic. The last person on earth he ever wanted to see again.

Even Guerro's excellent food wasn't worth being anywhere near Vic. Seb turned on his heels and began walking the other way.

"What's the hurry? I'm glad to see you," Vic called after him, following. "Been too long."

"Actually, not long enough." It was pointless to think he wouldn't run into the man at some point. There was a time when Seb had been one of Vic's best customers, meeting in the parking lot behind the train station to score pills no doctor would prescribe. The yank back to that old life nearly gave him whiplash.

"I heard you were clean now. Good for you." Vic's tone made a lie of those words. He wasn't pleased at Seb's recovery at all, and likely rooted against it at every turn.

"Excellent for me," he said, speeding up his steps. The irrational—well, maybe not so irrational—urge to run itched in his calves.

Vic did the running, dashing beside and then ahead of Seb to stand in front of him on the sidewalk. Were it not for a set of oncoming cars, Seb would have veered into the street to bypass him.

Vic held up his hands in false reassurance. "Hey, hey, slow down there. No hard feelings. I'm happy for you, man."

Seb skipped the polite "Thanks" and kept walking. There was a candle store two doors down, and despite zero interest in making a purchase, he'd duck in there just to get out of Vic's crosshairs.

Vic was walking backward ahead of him, ducking his head around to stay in Seb's field of vision. "How are you? Happy? Doing okay? Off the stuff for real?"

Seb knew what that meant. *If you're looking, I'm selling.* In a cruel twist, the pace of Seb's steps made him catch a toe on a bump in the sidewalk. The resulting jerk off balance sent a searing zing up his back. He winced.

Vic saw it. "Ah, not so good, huh?"

"Fine." Seb ground the word through his teeth, brandishing it like a shield against the false friendship in Vic's eyes. He hated the way his stabbing back made him limp a bit, and he continued on his way toward the shop. *Just get inside. Just get away from him.*

"I'm always here for you, Seb. You remember that. The time's coming when you're gonna want to remember that. And I'll be here. Right where you know to find me." Vic's tone was low and soothing. The easy sales pitch of a man who knew addiction did the selling for him.

Seb merely grunted, not caring that he nearly lunged at the shop door to yank it open—despite the jolt of pain it sent down his side—and threw himself inside.

"Well, hello, there." A singsong voice came from the woman behind the counter. She stared at him. "You okay?"

Seb forced himself upright, taking in a few deep breaths to command his muscles to stand down.

"Everyone always does that when they come in here," the woman said. She mistook the purpose of his deep breaths, but that was just fine with him. It did smell pretty good in there. A bit thick and sweet, but better than the stench Seb was sure surrounded Vic, who stood outside, staring in the windows.

The woman followed Seb's gaze to Vic. "You sure you're okay? Your friend doesn't look friendly out there."

"He's not my friend, and he's not friendly." Seb glared as hard as he could through the shop window, his dark message at odds with the cozy scents of the candle shop. "Just give me a minute, will you?"

"Absolutely." She agreed with a tsk and a shake of her head. "He looks like trouble. Makes me wonder if he's from that new camp up the mountain. I hear they're in town today."

So much for the warm welcome of scented candles. Rather than attempt any conversation, Seb just tried to be thankful for the safe harbor. He kept up his glare, steady and unblinking as a predator, until Vic finally gave up, shrugged and walked away.

They were both relieved when Vic was out of sight. Were he in a better place—in less pain and not spooked by the reappearance of Vic in his life—Seb might have tried to gain some ground for Camp True North Springs. Today just wasn't going to be that day.

For lack of any other idea on what to do next, Seb looked around the shop. "Have you got anything that smells like lemon meringue pie?"

He walked out of the shop a few minutes later, ashamed that he looked around to make sure Vic was nowhere in sight. *Don't give him that power*, he lectured himself. *He only has the power you give him.* He sent up a quick prayer that God could somehow keep Vic from his path for the rest of the day. The hard part was over. They'd met for the first time since he'd gotten clean. The shock would be easier to push past the next time…and somehow he knew there would be a next time.

"Quit it!" a familiar voice called out from the alleyway behind him, and Seb realized he'd been standing at the head of the alley that ran behind the block where the hardware store was.

"Will not. You're one of those camp kids, aren't you?" Seb heard the sound of a scuffle and moved closer.

"I said *quit* it!" He recognized the voice as Kent's. What was Kent doing nearly a block from the hardware store? Who'd let him wander off?

He discovered two much bigger boys shoving Kent into the alcove where the grocery store kept its dumpsters. Anger took the adrenaline still running through him and turned it into rage. Nobody—especially someone that age—should be giving a camp kid a hard time. Immediately, Seb grabbed the collar of the nearest bully and yanked him away from Kent. "What do you think you're doing?" he roared, not taking care to curb his tone. Before the kid could even reply, Seb grabbed the arm of the second kid and sent him careening against the dumpster.

The pair had to be at least fourteen, and old enough to know what they were doing was way out of line.

"Who're you?" the larger one barked, coming at him.

"The last person you want to mess with," Seb replied, snagging the kid's arm to twist it behind his back and pin him against the dumpster. That sent the smaller of the pair backpedaling out of Seb's reach.

"You okay?" he asked Kent, heartsick to see a scrape on the boy's arm and a mixture of fear and anger in his eyes.

"Sort of," Kent mumbled.

The smaller one took two steps toward the mouth of the alley, but Seb angled himself and his captive to block his exit. "Don't even try it." He put all the intimidation he knew into the command. "Into the hardware store. Now."

At just that moment Mike's son Rob came dashing out the hardware store's back door. "Kent! What were you…" His voice trailed off into a disgusted grunt as he took in the situation.

Seb grabbed the second boy and held tight to both of them. "Who are these boys?"

"Tucker Nicholson and Jeff Waden," Rob said. "I'd expect better of the two of you."

Seb recognized the last names as belonging to the two families that had put up the biggest fight against Camp True North Springs. Now the child-sized strong-arm tactics made sense. He could only imagine what these kids might be hearing from their parents at home, and it made his blood boil. He kept his grip on both boys, giving them an unfriendly shake. "Apologize. Now."

"I will not," said Tucker. "We live here. They don't."

Kent cowered against the building. That mean swipe at people who ought to be treated as welcome guests cut through any patience Seb had left. "I said apologize!" he commanded, shaking the boys enough that both of them yelped. It should bother him that his grip probably hurt them, but his temper had left the county.

"Let's not let things get out of hand," Rob said, looking slightly panicked. "I'm sure they didn't mean any harm."

Everyone in the alley knew that for the lie that it was. Seb was about to call them out on it when a voice bellowed behind them.

"Unhand my nephew!" Arthur Nicholson demanded, stabbing a finger at Seb. Of course the younger of the two boys in his grip was none other than the nephew of North Spring's least likable citizen. It made perfect sense where Tucker had gained his terrible view of the camp. Few people in town were more opposed to the opening of Camp True North Springs than Arthur Nicholson. He had never gotten over the defeat Dana and Mason had handed him when the town zoning board out-voted Arthur to allow the variance that made the camp possible.

Tucker jerked his arm out of Seb's grasp with a superior sniff that made Seb want to growl.

"This boy causing trouble?" Arthur asked, clearly meaning Kent.

Kent said nothing, just kept trying to melt into the brickwork and disappear.

Seb pointed a finger at Tucker. "*This* boy's causing trouble. Kind of you to pass on your oh-so-open mind about anyone from Camp True North Springs to every branch of your family, Art. What a welcome."

"He hurt me, Uncle Art," the boy whined. He was far too old and large to be whining, but he clearly knew how to play his uncle. Seb ground his teeth and tried to pull his hands out of the fists they were currently making.

"Me, too. He grabbed me and threw me against the dumpster, Mr. Nicholson." The second boy, Jeff, rubbed his shoulder as if wounded.

"Is anyone going to ask if *Kent* is okay?" Seb leveled a glare at Arthur.

"I think it's best you leave right now," Arthur said.

And here Seb was actually letting himself start to believe the possibility he was welcome here. That his future really could lie in North Springs. But with people like Arthur Nicholson around, who was he kidding?

Arthur sneered as he collected the two boys behind him, puffing up like a righteous protector. "I knew this would never work. I knew there was no place for this type of thing here."

Arthur left no doubt that "this type of thing" really meant "you."

Ten minutes later, Kate had been pulled out of the Gingham Pocket and was now standing with Dana, Mason, Kent and Seb, trying to work out what to do next. Kate bounced her gaze between Kent and Seb, reeling from the fallout of what had just happened. Her lovely treasure of a day had evaporated into thin air.

"All you did was make it worse," Mason said, his head in his hand as he sat on the seats that lined the gazebo. "You made Arthur's point for him."

Dana had filled Kate in on Arthur's role in the fight against Camp True North Springs. Even today, she had caught the stares from a few residents. Rita and a host of others had been warm and wonderful, but it was clear not everyone in North Springs felt the same way.

Seb was crackling like a live wire, pacing the gazebo. "You can't expect me to stand there and do nothing. They looked ready to lay into Kent. No way was I going to let that happen."

Kate looked down at the scrape on Kent's arm and the awful, sorrowful curl of Kent's small shoulders. Maybe it was wrong to have come here. It wasn't a reprieve—it was just another opportunity to be labeled as a trauma-survivor family.

Dana was in damage control mode, moving about the gazebo with low tones and efficient gestures. "You let your emotions get the better of you. All the staff are ambassadors for the camp when we come into town." She sent a supportive glance Kate's way. "We owe that to our guests."

"I want to go home," Kent said softly, rubbing his arm. "Where's Kimmy? Can't we just go home?"

The wounded whine in her son's voice cut Kate like a blade, and it did worse to Seb. He looked like he was falling apart, a giant ball of pain, regret and anger. Of course, he was wincing and rubbing his back—she had no doubt the stress was sending his muscles into knots. His heart as well, from the looks of it.

"Kimmy's with Mrs. Salinas at the Gingham Pocket, finishing up her flowerpot." As startled and worried as she was when Mason came to let Dana know what had happened, Kate was trying to salvage the outing for Kimmy by letting her finish the art project. And keeping the young girl out of this difficult conversation.

Seb stopped his pacing. "I'm sorry, Dana. Mason. I'm sorry I hurt the camp, really I am. But honestly, the way those boys were acting, I'd do it again. I won't let them talk like that about Kent. Or anyone. I just won't." After a heartbreaking pause, he said softly, "Maybe I'm just not ready to do this."

Mason put his hand on Seb's shoulder. "None of us are really ready. We're just doing the best we can. Nothing about this has been easy. It probably won't be for a while yet— if ever."

"And I just made it harder," Seb admitted, his voice sounding as wounded as Kent's.

"Maybe," Dana said. "But it was for all the right reasons." She cast her eyes around the grassy town square. "Maybe town outings aren't the thing to do just yet."

"So I ruined it for everybody," Kent moaned.

That sent Seb rushing to hunch at Kent's feet. "No, no, you've got it all wrong. *They* ruined it. Me, too, by the way I acted. But none of this—*none of this*—is on you. You got that, buddy?"

Kate's heart pinched at Seb's emotional plea on behalf of her son. Kent had been so quick to feel like the world was out to get him, as if life would never be happy for him. In the past few days that dark shell had begun to come off him, revealing the sweet boy he'd been before Cameron's death. She couldn't ignore how much Seb had been part of that renewal. Now it was as if Kent was a turtle, retreating back into his hard, dark shell with no plans of coming out ever again.

Seb grabbed Kent's hand. "I need to know you got that. I need to know I've still got my chili cook-off partner. No fair to let this mess that up."

Kent made no reply. Kate wanted him to say "Okay," but she knew her son. She could see the retreat already darkening his eyes. There would be no putting this to rights today. Maybe tomorrow, or the day after, but not today. Kent was right; there really wasn't anything to do now but go back to the camp. He'd want to go all the way home, but Kate wasn't ready to surrender all the progress they'd made. Seb was right about one thing: it was not fair to let this mess everything up.

"Thankfully, we took our own car. No need to cut short everyone else's day. But I think it's time we went back to the camp," Kate said quietly.

Dana's efficiency kicked into high gear as she held out her hand to Mason for the bus keys. "Why don't you and Seb see what you can square away with Mike at the hardware store. I'll walk with Kate and Kent back to Rita's to collect Kimmy. We'll decide what to do about Arthur and the boys when we've all got clearer heads about this."

Kate, Dana and Kent walked down the gazebo steps toward the bed-and-breakfast.

"I'll have Mr. Mason bring your birdhouse back from the hardware store," Dana said. "You can finish it back in the camp woodshop, okay?"

Kent only shrugged, his head down as he walked. *How could You let this happen, Lord?* Kate cried out from her wounded heart. *Don't let him go back to the sad and worried little boy who came here.*

"Mommy!" Kimmy gleefully held up hands smothered in pink paint when they walked onto the front porch. "I painted!"

Tina Caldridge turned around to point at the wide swath of pink on her cheek. "A lot, actually."

"I gots it all over," Kimmy said as if this were an accomplishment.

"I think your cleanup job is a bit harder than mine," Rita said, nodding to Dana. "Arthur's nephew, huh?" She motioned Kent toward her husband, who was coming out of the bed-and-breakfast's front doors. "Bart, why don't you take this young man into the kitchen and see if you can interest him in a brownie or two."

Bart gave a warm smile. "No one has to ask me twice. Come on, son, let's go put a dent in Mrs. S's stock of goodies."

"I'll take Kimmy in to wash up," Tina said. "Both of us need it."

Rita gestured toward the set of cushioned chairs on the porch. "I wish I could say I was surprised. Arthur will make a fuss about this. Seb ought to know better than to rise to that man's bait."

"He cares a lot about your son," Dana said. Her tone implied that Seb might not have reacted quite so harshly for any other camper. She wasn't wrong. Kate was sure everyone could see the special affection Seb had for Kent. She just hoped everyone couldn't see the attraction growing between Seb and herself.

Kate dared to say, "I think it's more than that. Something happened. Something else, I mean."

She would never admit to the strengthening bond between them, but she couldn't ignore the sense that something was off with Seb. Something more than just the insults of a couple of rude boys. He looked deeply shaken. Her gut told her something had pushed Seb to his edge even before he walked into that alley.

"What? Did he tell you something?" Dana asked.

"No, it's just a—" it felt dangerous to admit the connection she felt to him "—mother's intuition?"

"This is out of character for him. He's not a hot-temper kind of guy usually. I just figured he was tense on account of the conflict with the boys, but you're right, it could be something else."

"You've every right to ask him," Rita said. "You're his boss."

"Which is probably the reason why I shouldn't ask him. He's acting threatened." Dana looked at Kate. "He's more likely to open up to someone else."

Kate swallowed hard. She wasn't at all sure that someone ought to be her.

Chapter Nine

Seb stood in the kitchen doorway Sunday, saying the most fervent prayer he'd said in months. Everyone else was down at the church service. Mason thought it best the other families continue with that plan, but everyone agreed it was best for Kate, Kimmy and Kent to stay back, and Dana did as well.

In an effort to salvage anything he could, Seb had decided that the morning was a good time to cook up a trial batch of Kent's chili in preparation for the cook-off. It wasn't the most brilliant of plans, but he couldn't let Kent revert back to that solemn little guy and this was the only idea he had. *Let him come, Lord. Don't let me have messed this up.*

He was weary and achy. It had been an uneasy night, tossing and turning. The easy invitation in Vic's eyes stalked his thoughts and invaded his dreams. The wounded look in Kent's eyes when he asked if he could just go home—bail on the outing that was supposed to be the fun place where he could show off his talent—dug into Seb's gut and left it in knots. Seb was running out of optimism that this whole amazing setup would actually work out for him. And not just for him, but for Kent. For Kate. Even for Kimmy. Was the world that generous with second chances? Was God?

He knew what Mason and Dana would say to that, but Mason and Dana hadn't messed up on the monumental level he had. Either this would all work out, or it wouldn't. And Seb didn't know what he'd do if it didn't. He hadn't realized how much of his life was riding on the camp and his place in it.

Right now, it felt like the whole world depended on one ten-year-old boy walking into a kitchen and making chili.

Seb stared at the door of the barn dormitory, willing it to open. It didn't.

At a loss for what else to do, he walked back to the counter and began chopping onions. *Start without him*, he told himself. *Start like he'll show, and maybe he will.* At least, if nothing else, he could blame the onions for the angry tears threatening behind his eyes.

He got halfway through the first onion when he heard the click of the kitchen door behind him. His whole body stilled, gushing with hope that it was Kent and terrified that it wasn't.

"No fair, starting without me," Kent said in a small voice.

Seb almost teared up—okay, maybe not just almost—at the relief of Kent's voice and the absolution of the boy's arrival. He shut his eyes for a moment and forced a casual expression on his face before he turned. "Totally fair when you're late." He tossed an apron at Kent. "Wash up, Chef Kent. We've got to be done before any of the other families get back and get a whiff of the winning batch."

The grin on Kent's face was the best thing Seb had seen in ages. "'Cuz we're gonna win, right?"

"'Cuz we're gonna win," Seb replied. He nodded at the scrape on Kent's arm. "That okay?"

Kent flexed his arm. "Hurts a bit. Mom fussed over it. That's why I was late."

That was a far more welcome reason than "I didn't want to come anymore." Seb reached for the first aid kit in one of the cabinets, ignoring the zing of pain his back sent him for the effort. "Moms are supposed to fuss. Let's get a few more bandages on that just to make sure you don't get anything in there. She'll be impressed."

Kate. He hadn't talked to her since the whole business yesterday, even though he'd wanted to. He had no right to ask her to help him sort through the storm of his feelings, no right to bring her into his problems. Still, some part of him just knew he'd find his way through if he could talk to her about it. He liked the person he was when she was around—and he didn't much like himself this morning.

After applying two more bandages on the boy, Seb pushed the collection of bean and tomato cans over to Kent and handed him a can opener. "Get started on those while I finish this chopping, okay? There's a stool there so you can get a good angle and some leverage on it."

They worked in companionable silence for a few minutes before Seb asked, "How's your mom?"

"Mom," Kent moaned, as if the one word said everything. "She's getting all lecturey again. Stuff I need to learn, stuff I have to ignore, a gazillion *'life lessons I need.'"* He gave the final words a set of air quotes and an eye roll.

"Again, that's what moms are supposed to do." *Trust me, kid. Too much care is way better than nowhere near enough.* Maybe if his own mother had cared enough to shove a few life lessons down his throat at Kent's age, he wouldn't have ended up where he did. Where he was.

Kent got the last can open just as the ground beef and onions were finished cooking. They dumped the contents into the saucepan and gave it all a thorough stir. After adding the spices, Seb decided it was okay to ask the all-important question. "Are you mad at me?"

Kent looked up at him, and Seb felt his heart squeeze tight. "At you?"

"I didn't act in the smartest way. I made things worse. And I'm sorry for that. It's okay if you're mad at me about it." It had taken him hours to come up with the right way to say those four sentences. He had to get this right, for Kent's sake and for his.

Kent stared at him. Only, it wasn't a stare, it was something softer. Something small and vulnerable, something that broke Seb's heart wide open. "It was cool."

Seb grimaced. "But I didn't do the right thing. It wasn't cool."

Kent shrugged. "It was to me. Nobody's ever stood up for me like that. Like I had my own personal warrior dude. They were scared of you. That made me feel better."

Personal warrior dude. The title made Seb smile even if it wasn't a good life lesson. "I *am* your personal warrior dude, kid. Count on it. But you shouldn't need one, and I could have been way smarter in how I went about it. I got the camp into trouble."

"I know." The unspoken "but I'm glad you did it for me" made Seb want to take on the whole world for Kent's sake. "Thanks," the boy said, and put his arm around Seb's chest. Seb felt the closest thing to worthy he'd felt in years. He hadn't messed things up beyond repair. Things just might turn out okay.

Seb swallowed the king-size lump in his throat and said, "Check the recipe and see what comes next."

Kent's eyes lit up. "The secret ingredients come next. You got 'em?"

Seb played at being insulted. "Of course I got 'em." He walked over to a lower cabinet where he'd hid the secret ingredients to Cameron Hoyle's World-Famous Chili. Seb reached into the brown bag and pulled them out with superspy drama. "Two kinds of hot sauce, extra-hot chili powder, unsweetened baker's chocolate and coffee."

"Awesome!" Kent shouted, then clamped his hand over his mouth as if his declaration might be heard all the way down in North Springs. "You got the right ones and everything."

"Of course I did." Seb felt a beaming smile spread across his face. "Only the best for the Awesome Chili Chef Dudes."

Together they measured and added the secret ingredients, talking and whispering about their certain victory at the upcoming contest.

Kent gave a small leap, raising his ladle like an Olympic torch. "We're gonna win!" he declared.

Seb was taking a breath to join in the cheer when Kent's leap tilted toward the stove. The breath turned into a yell of alarm as Kent instinctively put his hand out to steady himself, grabbing the handle of the enormous pot without thinking.

Time slowed down to terrible details. Kent's face changed from joy to pain as the heat of the handle seared his palm. The pot tilted toward the edge of the stove. Seb dove for the pot, one hand landing on the side of it to push its fall away from Kent while the other pulled Kent toward him out of danger. The resulting twist sent a surge of fire down Seb's spine, as if a dozen of the kitchen's sharpest knives were embedded in his back.

Kent cried out as he fell back out of the way. Seb hit the ground with a shattering thud he seemed to feel in every bone of his body. He tried to muffle his scream as the world went white, but he failed.

A loud metallic crash and a cascade of yelling startled Kate out of the conversation she'd been having on the porch with Dana, who'd stayed behind from church as well. Kimmy was playing with clay next to her on the swing. Seconds later Kent burst out from the house, wide-eyed and grabbing his hand. "It's Seb!" he gulped out between panicked sobs. "He's hurt. Bad."

Dana shot out of the chair toward the kitchen while Kent grabbed Kate's arm with his good hand and began tugging her in the same direction.

They found Seb flat on the floor, stiff and

hissing through his teeth. Beyond his head the enormous pot lay on its side, spilling chili out like a tipped volcano in the center of a ring of splatters.

"He pushed me out of the way," Kent said, alternating between panting and crying. "He's hurt, Mom. He's not gonna die, is he?"

The question cut through Kate like a blade. Did Kent now think every accident ended in someone dying?

"Not. Dead." Seb strained to get the words out through clenched teeth. His hands were braced flat on the floor beside him, knuckles nearly white.

Not dead, no, but clearly in excruciating pain. Dana raced to the office to call 911. It might take a while for them to get up the mountain—Kate had to do something. She knelt down beside him. Frightened by the scene, Kimmy scrambled onto her lap and held tight. With one hand, Kate held Kimmy, while she laid the other on Seb's hand. He sucked in a sharp breath and she could feel the tendons of his hand pushing against the floor.

"Breathe," she said, knowing there was nothing else she could do just yet. "Get in one good breath. Come on, you can do it."

He didn't open his eyes. His jaw was set like iron.

"In," she coaxed, rubbing his hand. Seb pulled in a short, tortured breath. Kate felt herself breathing alongside him, for him. "Out."

His exhale came in spurts, tightening into a hiss she could see in the spasms of his chest and shoulders. It didn't take a medical degree to see what had happened.

Dana came barreling through the kitchen door behind her, phone still in hand. "I've called the paramedics. It'll be about five minutes for them to come from town, but I'll have the gate open when they arrive." She looked down at Seb, her features filling with pity and concern. "Hang in there, Seb. Help is on the way. Don't move."

"No. Chance." Seb ground out the words, teeth still clamped shut.

"In," Kate cued again, making a small circle with her hand on the back of his palm. Kimmy began to cry. Seb turned his hand over to clasp hers, so tightly she almost cried out herself, but instead she held tight. "Out."

"What about you? Let's get a cold cloth on that hand," Dana said, reaching for Kent's hand.

Kent yanked his hand out of Dana's grasp. "I'm fine!"

He wasn't, but Kate knew that wasn't a battle she was going to win right now. Kent was back in crisis mode, and she could almost see the fear coursing through him. He needed something to do, some useful action to knock him out of the shock threatening to swallow him. "What do you say we get this mess cleaned up?" She tried to slip her hand from Seb's, but he held on tight and opened his eyes to look at her with a desperate pleading. He was struggling not to cry out, and she knew it was for Kent's and Kimmy's sake.

"C'mon, Kent, help me," Dana said, righting the pot and grabbing a pair of spatulas to begin scraping the meaty mixture from the floor.

The next ten minutes were a blur of noises, lights, shouts. Seb finally released her hand as the paramedics crowded into the kitchen, but his last look into her eyes burrowed deep into Kate's chest.

Pain—real pain—was never just a feeling. It was visible, hovering behind eyes and radiating off faces. Most times Kate could muster a sense of purpose when faced with such pain, a calling to heal. Every once in a while a glimpse of terrible pain would leave her feeling helpless, powerless against a wall of suffering too high to break down.

Finally, Kent allowed Dana to pull him to the other side of the kitchen under the guise of washing his hand and putting a cold compress on the blistering burn rising on the heel of it.

It could have been so much worse. The steam rising off the chili told her the pot had been boiling when it had been knocked over. Had Seb not lunged and pushed the pot away, they both could have been badly burned. They weren't, but Seb had paid a high price for that outcome.

Dana came over and said quietly, "They need to move him. How about we get Kent and Kimmy out of here before that happens?" Kate read her "out of earshot" without a word being spoken.

Kate took her son by his good hand and hoisted Kimmy onto her hip. "Let's go change your shirt. We'll come back and see Seb in a bit, okay?"

"I'll be fine, kid," Seb grunted, breathing hard. Sweat beaded on his forehead. "Just a scratch." No one believed him. Not even Kent. Still, Kate's heart twisted at the effort Seb was making.

She looked back just for a second as Kent was out the door, catching the wild, panicked look in Seb's eyes. Whatever they were going to do to him next, it would hurt. Beyond words. She said a small prayer that he might pass out, just to spare him whatever agony came next.

And whatever agony came after that.

Chapter Ten

If Kate got any sleep, it wasn't much.

Kent lay curled beside her on her bed, fit-fully dozing. Some acetaminophen and oint-ment had dulled the throb Kent complained about in his palm, but not enough. She imag-ined that for him, like for her, the site of an ambulance's flashing lights driving away with someone inside took his imagination to dark places. Trauma seemed like such a gentle word for all the stabs and aches of their cata-strophic memories. One trauma never seemed able to separate itself from another—they all just piled on each other, pressing down harder with each new addition.

Just before dawn—it must have been 5:00 a.m. or so—Kate heard the sound of the gate opening and the beams of car lights coming down the drive. Mason—and, she hoped, Seb—must be coming back from the hospital. She strained to hear Seb's voice, but couldn't. The shuffle of slow footsteps and the mutter of muffled voices, however, gave her hope that he'd returned. She prayed that his injuries hadn't been severe enough to require that he be admitted for inpatient treatment.

That wasn't necessarily a good thing. Hospitals had options for pain control that often couldn't be used in an outpatient setting. And someone with Seb's history? Well, that complicated things further. While opiates were powerfully useful when properly administered in severe cases for short durations, none of those options were open to Seb. The likely truth was that Seb was in a lot of pain, and would be for a while. There was a wild fear that filled his eyes in his final glance to her as they loaded the gurney into the ambulance. It stayed fixed in her memory, pushing sleep far out of reach.

She couldn't get up, not with Kent finally asleep beside her. She couldn't hope to fall back asleep herself, tired as she was. She couldn't do anything.

Except pray. She could pray. There was always that, no matter where she was or whatever words eluded her.

Help us, she prayed, admitting she and Kent needed God's grace and protection as much as Seb at the moment. *Ease his pain. Calm his fears. Hold him in the palm of Your hand. Us, too. He means a lot to me. He means too much to me. Only You know what's best here.*

Kate prayed until the sun crept its way through the windows and Kimmy woke. Breakfast would be soon—but made by whom? Even as used to working in pain as he was, Kate doubted Seb would be back in the kitchen anytime soon.

She washed, dressed herself and Kimmy, and gently shook Kent awake at the last minute. Kimmy chattered in her usual way as they walked across the grass to the big house and the dining room, but she and Kent were quiet.

Her son stopped at the announcement board that stood at the foot of the steps. Kate's heart pulled small and tight as Kent stared at the poster for the chili cook-off. Would it even happen now? Would anyone have the heart to go on with the event once they had learned of the accident? It seemed so wrong for all of Kent's creative artwork to have been in vain.

"I really like your posters," Kate said, just

because she couldn't let the weight of the moment stay pressing down on them. The morning felt cold and dark despite the bright sunshine and the heat that was already building.

With a grunt that sounded like it belonged on an old man, Kent yanked the poster from the pins that held it in place. The tiny ripping sound echoed hugely across the silence of the yard.

Kate held out her hand for the poster, worried Kent would drop it to the ground. "We've still got more time here. We might be able to have it, just a bit later."

"Why?" Kent moaned. Clearly, he considered the event ruined forever. Kate worried that he might be right. *Is there any way to save this, Lord?*

She didn't have a good answer for Kent's doubts. At least not yet. So she opted for, "At least you should keep one of the posters. It's good work."

He handed it to her without a word or the slightest hint of pride. Using his bandaged hand, no less. The brightening boy she'd begun to see earlier had all but disappeared. Could he find his way back in the time they had left at camp?

Kimmy tugged on her arm. "Cheffub

okay?" The way she wrapped her tiny mouth around her version of Seb's name tightened Kate's throat.

She cast her glance over to the building where she knew Seb's room was. "We don't know yet, sweetheart. I'm sure the doctors made things better." Did they? Could they? There seemed to be little signs of life or movement in the small cottage. *Let him be sleeping*, she prayed, *or at least resting.* The urge to go see him, to do whatever she could for him, rose up.

Ah, but that might not be the smartest thing right now. Her emotions were raw and vulnerable. Kent and Kimmy shouldn't be close to the situation—or, at least Seb—until things had calmed down. Every speck of common sense told Kate it was best to leave this to Dana and Mason for now. Trouble was, she didn't feel at all like listening to common sense.

"Hello, froggy!" Kimmy called, and waved at Franco and his fountain as they walked toward the porch stairs.

Kate applied the rally cry that had helped her crawl through the early days of Cameron's loss, and each of the many crises since: *Do the thing in front of you.* Kate reached down for Kimmy's hand. "Let's go get breakfast." Straightening her shoulders, she mounted the porch steps toward Dana's voice coming from the dining room. So Dana was manning the kitchen, with help from Rose Caldridge and her girls, it sounded like. Life in Camp True North Springs was finding a way to keep going. After all, keeping on in a crisis was familiar territory for all the camp families, wasn't it?

Later today, she'd find a way to visit Seb. She told herself it was so that she could give an update to Kimmy and Kent, but even she didn't believe that was the whole reason.

It hurt.

It hurt to breathe, to move. It felt like it hurt to think.

It is better, he struggled to remind himself. The white-hot stab of the initial fall had settled into a hard grip that held him prisoner on his bed. He hadn't spent this much time staring at the ceiling since the early days of rehab.

And that was the biggest trouble right there—these were old wounds. Physically, mentally, emotionally, spiritually. *I am a different man than the one who crashed that motorcycle*, he told himself as he adjusted the ice pack underneath him. *I'm not back there. I won't go back there.*

That was easy enough to say, but he knew that every passing hour of the pain level he currently endured might make it harder to hold on to that conviction. *You've got to help, Lord. You've got to throw a big wide moat of protection around me.* He thought of the "you'll come around" look in Vic's eyes and felt another piece of his confidence crumble.

There came a gentle knock on the door. Seb didn't like his initial, irrational impulse to check the clock in the hope it was time for another dose of the nowhere-near-strong-enough pain medicine they'd sent home with him. Even though it wasn't anything even close to a narcotic, he'd given it to Dana, absurdly frightened to keep it in his own possession.

Lying here gave him far too much time to worry. About Kent. About Kate. About the camp and how much he'd made things worse with Arthur Nicholson. About the future of this job he'd come to love. About his future, period.

It was Kate. He'd never been so glad to see anyone in his life.

"Hi," she said, her soft voice seeming to fill the room. "Up for a visit?"

Seb was almost desperate enough to admit he'd been counting the hours until she would come see him. He'd been thinking of her, of what it felt like to have her hold his hand. The sensation was firm and vivid in his memory. Did she know how much she'd helped him at that desperate moment? How her touch was the one thing that helped him breathe? To fight against the impulse to tense up and panic?

"You betcha," he replied, trying not to sound as relieved as he was. "Forgive me if I don't get up."

"You stay right where you are," she said, that "do as you're told" tone he found so amusing coloring her voice. She took the chair from his desk and pulled it up next to the bed. He was so grateful to have her close. "I'd ask you to rate your pain on a scale of one to ten—" her smile was a kind of tender that sunk deep into his chest "—but I expect you've answered that a dozen times so far."

He rounded down. "Seven. Until I move the wrong way, then about fourteen."

"Were they able to give you something?" He welcomed her careful tone. It told him she knew the complexity of that question. And the stakes involved.

"Something. Not enough. But...considering..." Seb didn't have the energy to say out loud what they both already knew. Most of the drugs able to handle his current level of pain were danger zones for him. He hoped his resolve held out. Part of him was afraid to be alone with his thoughts right now. "I'm glad you're here," he ventured. "I could use the company."

God must have heard his unspoken plea, for she wrapped her hand around his. "I'll stay as long as I can."

The soft cool of her hands was the most amazing thing he'd felt in years. Maybe forever. He let his fingers nestle against hers, unable to care if he held on too tightly. He needed the lifeline of her presence too much to care whether or not it was wanted or wise. He closed his eyes, too afraid of the way he'd look at her if he left them open.

"Seb," she said gently after a second. "You're holding your breath. That only makes it worse. Come on, breathe. In...out...just like before."

He let her guide his breaths, slowing them down, undoing the tension so that he could take deeper breaths. Of course it helped. Her voice allowed him to pull apart the knots and barbs inside so that they ached rather than stabbed. Her fingers made soft, soothing circles on the back of his palm that radiated up his arm. His heartbeat kept repeating *I need you* so clearly Seb was worried he'd say it out loud if he wasn't careful.

"How is Kent?" he managed to ask, glad he could finally think past the wall of pain to the boy's welfare. "I'm so sorry I…" His words cut off to a hiss when he made the mistake of trying to turn toward her.

"Stop that," she said. "I should be thanking you. That pot would have come down on him if you hadn't lunged at it. You saved him." Her voice caught on that last bit, and she gave a hard swallow. "And now look at you. You're a hero, you know that?"

He didn't feel anything like a hero. Still, Seb let himself hang on to the gratitude in her voice. "So he's okay?"

Her hands tightened around his. "His thumb and hand is burned. And he's upset. About you, and about the chili cook-off being canceled. But mostly about you."

That regret came close to aching as much

as his back. "I ruined what should have been his big moment."

"You protected my son," she shot back, shaking his hand a bit with each word. "I can't thank you enough." A mother's protective passion filled her voice. Kent and Kimmy had someone who cared so much about them. He was envious of that—for more than one reason.

"That's good," he tried to joke, "'cause I hate to tell you this, but your pie's gonna have to wait a bit now."

She laughed, and he tried to as well—until his rib cage reminded him that was a supremely bad idea. Still, he wanted to see her, and life wouldn't hand him a better motivation to try to get upright. "Can you help me get up? Does the trick you taught me earlier work in extreme cases?"

She made a disapproving sound. "Are you sure? It's probably going to hurt."

"It hurts now," he retorted. "And I'm not going to get better expert help at this than you." He squeezed her hand. "Please. I want to try. If I can manage it," he admitted, "I'll know this won't get the better of me." He had to know he was stronger than the pain, and he couldn't think of anyone better to help him know that.

"Okay," she said warily. "But we're going to take this *very* slow."

If it kept her here longer, all the better. At least the pain would be worth something. "I'll follow orders exactly."

"Why do I get the feeling that's a rare occurrence?" He very much liked the affection in her voice. "All right then, deep breath, hold it while you roll toward me, then exhale."

He followed her instructions despite the cascade of fire it sent across his back. It did, however, allow him to look at her, and that was pretty fair compensation. Those dimples. The woman had a smile that could make a man cross a desert. Or an ocean. Or maybe, in this case, just roll over.

"How much did that hurt?" she asked, eyes narrowed in assessment.

"I refuse to say." He didn't quite keep the agony out of his voice. Seb lay there on his side for half a minute, letting the pain die down. When he was ready for the next step, he nodded.

"Okay," she said. "This is the harder part." She took his hand and guided it to the spot in front of his chest like she'd shown him in the garden. "Put your weight on your hand, like we did before." He'd been rising that way ever since she'd shown him the first time, so he didn't need her guidance, but it was nice to feel her touch on his hand again. "Same thing. Don't hold our breath. Inhale while you push up. It'll hurt, but don't let that make you rush. Ease through it slowly."

He gave her a narrow-eyed assessment of his own. "Easy for you to say."

It did hurt. A lot. But there was something victorious about being able to sit upright. It made him feel less damaged, less wounded. Standing would make him feel even better from a mental standpoint—but the physical cost might be whopping. Still, if she was beside him helping him, he could do it. Kate made things possible for him. What would he do once she'd left? He didn't even want to think about that now.

"You strike me as the impatient type, so let's not stand just yet. Sit for a minute."

The pause, while welcome, also gave him an idea. "Would you go over to that top drawer and take out the little white bag? While we're waiting and all."

She gave him a quizzical look, but walked over to his dresser and tugged open the top drawer. "This one?" she asked, holding up the bag from the candle shop in town.

Kate's eyebrows furrowed as he could tell she caught the lemon scent of the candle. "That's for you," he said, feeling a bit sheepish.

Her face showed a mix of pleasure and surprise at the gift, small as it was. "Me?" The smile she gave as she pulled out the lemon-scented candle was the best painkiller he could have.

Seb managed a shrug. "It made me think of you. And now I kind of owe it to you, deferred pie and all."

"You don't owe me," she said, eyes warm. "I owe you. Quite a bit."

He didn't see it that way. "How about we just call it even?"

She took a luxurious inhale of the candle's scent, and Seb felt the storm in his nerves ease up a bit with the deep breath he took alongside her.

"Thank you. But you may not call it even once we get you standing." She set the candle on Seb's bedside table. He liked how close it was, how he could pick up the scent from where he sat.

Kate held out both hands. "Okay. Load that

weight on those legs slowly. Let your back settle into it. And breathe. You've got this."

He wasn't quite sure he did, but the small zing that went through him when Kate took his hands did the convincing for him.

It took way longer than he liked, and hurt way more than he planned, but within a few minutes he was upright. Eventually the short, sharp gulps of air calmed down to steady breaths. As a prize, Seb let himself stare into the encouragement of her blue eyes.

The pain hadn't won. He was standing.

Kate nodded to the wall by the head of his bed. "Take a few small steps and let's get you leaning against the wall. It'll help you to stay steady. Small steps, deep breaths."

She helped him shuffle toward the wall and pivot until he could lean back against it. He closed his eyes and tilted his head back against the wall, a big exhale of relief whooshing from him.

"Good work," she encouraged. "Set those vertebrae against the wall and breathe from your belly. Tell me a story."

A story? Now? Maybe it was a therapist trick. Well, if he had her this close as a captive audience, he'd tell an important story. One that counted. "I'll tell you why I lost it on Kent's account. Why I…laid into those boys…probably more than I should have."

Kate pulled her hands from his and took a tiny step backward. "All right."

"His name is Vic. I saw him in town." The story came in short spurts as Seb held himself upright against the wall. She made no reply, only listened.

"A short bit before I saw Kent. It wasn't a happy reunion. I'd hoped I'd never see him again. He was delighted to see me." Seb gave a weighty pause. "I was one of his best customers."

It took Kate a moment to catch his meaning. "Your…?" she didn't know what word to use.

He did. "Dealer. Source. My good buddy with a full pharmacy in the back of his black van. Yeah, him."

"What did he want?"

"It wasn't to congratulate me on my recovery, if that's what you're asking." He didn't like admitting this, but she deserved to know why he'd gone off like a lit fuse when he'd seen those boys threaten Kent. "He wanted to make sure I knew I was welcome back anytime I wanted." Seb imitated Vic's predatory smile.

"Don't you dare go back," Kate said.

Her plea lodged in his heart and made him yearn to win his battle against this enemy. "You keep that up. I'm in need of a cheering squad here." He made a move to step toward her, but it triggered a spasm and he fell back against the wall with a sharp hiss of an inhale.

"In," she cued him, raising her hand to tell him to inhale while she held his gaze. There was so much swirling in her eyes. Even in the midst of his pain and fear, he could feel the heat of his dazzling attraction to her. "Out." Some brazen part of him hoped it was as much to calm her pulse as his.

She did it three more times. Seb did his best to hold her gaze even as sweat began to bead on his forehead. Just as he was sure he wouldn't last much longer, she pronounced, "All right, tough guy, I think you've been upright long enough. Get back on that bed."

Even though he was inwardly relieved, Seb stuck out his lower lip in a pout Kimmy would have envied. "Who's gonna make me?"

Kate gave him an "oh, grow up" glare but held out one forearm for Seb to use like a handlebar and pointed to the bed with her other hand.

He obediently went through the reverse of

the motions that took him upright. He tried not to wince or groan, not willing to admit they'd likely pushed things farther than they ought to have—on more than one level. He didn't want her to know it hurt worse now than when she'd arrived.

"Do you have to go?" He could tell the hint of weakness in his tone pulled at her.

"I need to get back to Kimmy and Kent. I'll bring them by later if you feel you're up to it. You hang in there. It will get better from here, and that's my professional opinion."

He rolled his face to look at her. "And what's your personal opinion?"

She squeezed his hand. "You're strong enough. And prayers are going up on your behalf."

Seb felt his strength and determination seep away in the wake of her exit. He let his head fall onto the pillow, hoping Kate was right on both counts.

Chapter Eleven

Kate kept her distance from Seb the next day. Things felt far too close between them, and she knew he'd try to do more than he ought to in her presence. He needed rest, not to show off to her. And she needed time to sort through the storm of feelings being with him rose up in her.

Distraction wasn't hard to find in the form of the new litter of kittens in the barn. Kimmy was fascinated with them, and their simple joy felt healing to watch. "I want one," Kimmy pleaded, not for the first time. "Can we have one?"

The kittens were cute. And small. And sweet. But not at all anything that could come home with them to Pennsylvania. Kate gave Kimmy a sympathetic smile as she sat on a nearby hay bale next to Heidi Boswell. "I know that sounds like it would be fun, but it's not something we can do right now, sweetheart."

Kimmy pouted. "I want one." She kept asking as if she'd wear Kate down with sheer persistence.

Heidi put the kitten she was holding in her lap down to frolic with the other two on the barn floor. Her sons wanted nothing to do with the cuteness of kittens, but Tina and Cindy Caldridge were playing with them alongside Kimmy. "It would be a long, hard journey home to your house, Kimmy. But the best part is you can play with them here as much as you like, right?"

Kate smiled at the "look on the bright side" mom effort Heidi was giving. Cindy was giving a long look to the kittens as well. "Mrs. Boswell is right. They'll be much happier here."

"Kent wants one, too," Kimmy said, lower lip firmly stuck out.

"And how do you know that?" Kate asked, one eyebrow raised in doubt. Like the Boswell boys, her son did not seem the kitten type, especially now if ever.

"I just know."

Heidi leaned back against the barn wall on the hay bales they'd been using as seats while the girls played on the straw floor with the kittens. "How is Kent?"

Kate sighed. It had been a long few days since the accident. "Brooding. I'm going to give him one more day of staying mostly in his room and then I'm going to have to drag him back out into the world, I think." She found herself second-guessing all sorts of decisions—parenting and otherwise—lately.

"Boys that age are champion brooders. It just gets worse, I hate to tell you." She paused for a moment before adding, "I always wondered if Doug would have eventually been happy at college. If we should have let him come home when he was struggling that first semester." She looked at Kate. "You rethink everything, you know? Wondering if maybe you'd have made this choice or that, then they'd still be with you."

The girls had gone farther away, following the kittens as they tumbled through the barn. Kate felt they were far enough out of earshot to ask, "Tell me about what happened? About your son?"

"Thank you," Heidi said. "No one gets why we need to be asked that." She looked around.

"Well, no one outside camp." She pulled in a deep breath. "The simple, awful truth is that Doug was in the wrong place at the wrong time. No fault, no mistake, just in the line of fire when some young man on campus decided his gun was the best way to show the world how angry he was. Doug and three others died, for no good reason other than they were right there, right then." She chewed on her lip, shoulders rising in the hold-it-together posture Kate knew all too well. "I can't make sense of it."

"There's no sense to make of it." Kate picked up a piece of hay and rolled it between her fingers. It smelled fresh and earthy, and she found that comforting. As if the world still knew how to grow things despite the horrors that kept happening. "Cameron took a shortcut to get home earlier and he never got home at all. It's senseless, all of it."

Heidi nodded at the girls. "Do you wonder if they'll ever heal? Them, my boys, your two—if they'll really, truly heal? Are you scared they'll just have this giant hole in their lives forever, like it feels now?"

It hurt to talk about it, but it helped, too. "Kimmy's grief will be different—the challenge will be to build a strong memory of

Cameron for her. Kent, I worry about. A boy needs his father at that age. But I lost my dad when I was sixteen, and I managed to make peace with it eventually."

The mama cat came wandering into the barn, sitting between Heidi and Kate in an amusing trio of motherhood all watching children play.

"But someone dying from an illness and having someone taken from you like...like Cameron and Doug..." Kate went on, "It's different. You feel like you can't count on anything in the world after that. Even God, for a while." She sighed and shook her head. "The things I said to our Lord on my bad days. I think I'm proof there really is endless grace. Receiving it, I mean. I'm not so great at showing it."

Heidi stroked the mama cat. "I want to stop hating him. The shooter. After all, he was in his own kind of torment. The logical part of me tells me he didn't get the help he needed. But my heart still blames him for taking Doug from me. I hear what you say about the things that go through your head on the bad days. I don't want to pass that on to my boys."

"I suppose that's why we're all here," Kate replied.

The cat jumped down to join the rumpus on the barn floor. Heidi gave Kate a careful look. "Can I ask what might be an awful question?"

Not quite sure how to answer, Kate said, "I think so."

"Do you think about…trying again? About how maybe you'll find someone else someday? You're young enough. It should happen for you."

Kate was keenly aware at that moment how irreplaceable a lost child was. Not that any death was ever replaceable, but while Kate could know the possibility of a new man to love someday, Heidi had no such chance to love a third son.

When she didn't answer, Heidi teased, "Come on. Every one of us has seen the way Seb looks at you. The way you're worried about him right now. Are you ready?"

It startled Kate to think Seb's affection was that obvious to other people. "Who's ever ready?"

"Granted, he's got a bit too much swagger for my taste, but you could do worse. And a man who cooks like that? I'm thankful if I can get Ron to make the morning coffee." She stretched, a bit of the previous sadness sloughing off her. That's how grief went—

coming and going in waves large and small. "The best part of this whole thing has been not cooking and doing dishes."

"We're only here for a short while. You know that." Kate had no business disclosing the reasons why Seb was an unwise choice even if she was ready and they lived closer. To them, he was simply a good cook and a good man. His private challenges should stay private until he chose to talk about them. And he was certainly in no place to do that now.

Heidi caught her hesitation. "He's okay, isn't he? They said he hurt his back. Is it bad? You're a physical therapist, can you tell?"

"He has a lot of healing to do." It was the truth. "I expect the next day or so will tell."

"Mom?"

Both women turned, surprised to find Kent standing behind them. Kate tried hard not to show how pleased she was to see her son out of his room. "Hi, kiddo. What's up?"

"I went to see Seb. Mason said I could."

Oh, to be a fly on that wall, Kate thought. "How is he?"

"Not so good, I think." Kent looked scared and worried. "Is he gonna be okay?"

That was a dangerous question to answer.

Instead, Kate opted for a question of her own. "What's got you so worried about him?"

"I think he hurts. A lot. He says he's fine but I think it's pretty plain he isn't. It's been two whole days. Are they gonna have to like operate on him or something? Did he break something in his back?"

At least this she could answer. "No. And they can tell with X-rays. It's just that the kind of injury Seb has causes a lot of pain." She watched Kent flinch at that. Try as she might, it was going to take a lot of time, prayer and talk to help Kent see that Seb's injuries weren't his fault. "It might take a bit of time."

Kent plopped down on the hay bale like a spindly scarecrow. "What if he's not better by the time we leave?"

She risked placing a hand lightly on Kent's shoulder. "I don't think that'll happen." Fishing for something more concrete for Kent to hang on to, she asked, "Was he sitting up when you were with him?"

"Yeah. Kind of. On his bed."

Kate's mind brought up the image of Seb's careful, determined battle to stand. Part of her yearned for such a fierce, fighting spirit.

"Well, that's more than he could do when I saw him. Sounds like he's improving."

Kent shook his head. "Yeah, well, I don't think so. Can't you do something?"

Lingering pain—and on the level Kent seemed to be describing—didn't bode well for Seb. The longer the pain went on, the longer relief eluded him. And that held all kinds of dangers for someone like Seb.

She'd been resisting making a certain suggestion, but maybe now was the time to show some fierce, fighting spirit of her own. "Actually, there might be something we can try. Let's go talk to Mason and see if he'll make a few calls."

Wednesday morning, Seb prided himself on making it to the big house to sit in one of the living room's overstuffed chairs. He tried to make it feel like rest. Everybody said "rest up," but Seb's mood was the total opposite of rest, and had been since that close call in the kitchen. Yesterday afternoon he decided he couldn't handle one more hour locked in his room, and gingerly began making short trips around the grounds.

It was slow going. Every part of him—body, soul, mood, spirit—ached. His whole being was raw and sore. But today he'd discovered that if he tucked the throw pillows on this one particular chair just so, it took the pain down to a five. Still, that made it barely worth being on display to all the camp families as they passed through this public space on their way to meals or other activities.

To be honest, enduring a steady stream of "How are you?"s and "Are you feeling better?"s was only slightly better than being isolated in his room.

How am I? Scared, full of doubts, worried the next accident will take me down for good. Am I feeling better? Ask me again in five minutes. Sunday had shown him that he could, at any time, be thrust back into the ocean of pain that threatened him with relapse. And that terrified him.

Where do I go from here, God? There's no safe place anywhere in sight. Will there ever be?

The only thing that kept him from retreating back to his room was the fact that Kate, Kimmy and Kent would likely pass through at some point. At lunch, if nothing else, but he hoped sooner than that. He desperately wanted to see them. Well, Kate mostly—and that was a worry of a whole other kind—

but time with any of them had become the high point of any day. *I'm in trouble here*, he warned the Almighty. *They mean too much to me. And we both know they're leaving.*

Seb tried hard not to think of what Camp True North Springs would feel like without the Hoyle family. It wouldn't be a grief like all the camp families had known, but Seb feared it would come close.

He was just shifting the pillow a third time when Kent burst into the living room carrying a box. "Come into the side room," Kent commanded as if he were in charge. "Mom's gonna plug you in." The side room was a narrow combination of a workroom and office with a long table where meetings were often held.

"If I were a toaster oven, maybe," Seb replied, wondering just what was going on.

Kimmy came in behind her brother, carrying a bed quilt nearly as big as she was. "You're not," she agreed, laughing at his poor joke. The tiny, cheerful giggle reminded Seb again what a delightful sound a child's laugh could be.

Kate came in behind her children, a determined look on her face that let Seb know he was getting out of that chair whether he liked it or not. "You are not a toaster oven. And I'm not going to plug you in. Not really. But electricity is involved."

"You mind explaining—" Seb paused for a moment as his back complained loudly at being roused off the pillows "—what that's supposed to mean?"

"I had Mason pull a few strings down at the medical center. We got you a TENS unit."

Kent hoisted the box up an inch or two to display it. "Come on."

Now even the kids were ordering him around. Those dimples let them get away with just about anything. Their mother as well, come to think of it. It was three against one, and he didn't stand a chance. He ought to have minded, but he couldn't quite muster up the annoyance.

"What's a TENS unit?" Seb asked as he followed the trio into the side room, irritated that he had to stop and lean against the doorway while a mean zing went down his spine. The urge to run that bubbled in his stomach wasn't much good given that he could only manage a slow walk this morning. Still, he was upright and moving. Too much like an old man, but moving nonetheless. That was progress.

"It's an electronic device that sort of short-circuits your nervous system. Like white noise for your pain sensors. Takes things down to a dull roar for lots of people who can't…access certain medications."

His eyes opened with a dark scowl. "Shock therapy for lost causes?" They had both stopped just short of using the word "addicts" in front of Kent and Kimmy.

"Inventive treatments for people who deserve a fighting chance," she corrected. Had Kate schemed to include them in this little escapade because she knew he wouldn't put up a fight in front of them? That woman was as wily as she was beautiful.

"That's you," Kimmy said with a heart-wrenching sincerity. The little girl raised herself up on tiptoes to hoist the quilt on the table. Whatever was going to happen, it now looked as if it involved him lying down on the side room table.

Seb was about to register his doubts when Kate shut the side room door. At least this spectacle wouldn't have spectators. "I'm not so sure about this," he said. "I've tried just about everything and nothing's really helped."

"It looks cool," Kent said, putting the box down on the room's long wooden console and taking a disturbing tangle of cords and electrical looking things out of the box. The boy caught Seb's dubious look and nearly rolled his eyes. "Mom says it doesn't hurt. Just the opposite. Only, I'm not sure how."

"What makes you think I'm in a hurry to find out how?"

"C'mon," Kent shot back, showing as much spunk as he'd seen from the boy in days. "You can't be afraid of whatever Mom does to you, can you?" He waved one of the white label-like squares at Seb as if to show that both it and his mother were incapable of harm.

Seb wasn't so sure. In his experience, many of those "this may cause a bit of discomfort" treatments hurt. A lot. He wasn't in the mood for a new dose of pain today.

Kate had been spreading the blanket over the table even though he had yet to give his consent. "It's not exactly a treatment table, but it's a better height than a bed or a sofa." She gave Seb a hopeful look. "Do you think you can get up on it and lie on your stomach?"

That definitely sounded like a painful process. Still, he wasn't going to admit it in front of Kate and her children. Hitting on a solution, Seb looked at Kent. "Tell you what. I'll do whatever this is if you agree to have a do-over for the chili cook-off."

That set Kent back a bit. The boy had retreated back into his shell since the accident and the cancellation of the event. It was time to reverse that, and the prospect would serve as a great incentive for however bad it hurt to climb up on this table and let Kate plug strange things into his skin.

He raised an eyebrow at Kent's hesitation and Kate's wary look. "C'mon, tough guy, what do you say?"

After a long uncertain moment, Kent muttered, "Sure."

Seb smiled at the victory and walked toward the table—until Kate held up one hand. "There is one thing. You'll have to take your shirt off. The pads go on your skin."

"Mom says it fizzes," Kimmy said. "Tickly." She wiggled her fingers.

Lying shirtless on a conference table in front of Kate Hoyle wasn't anything Seb would describe as "tickly." Intimate, but nothing close to romantic. Still, *very* interesting.

He chose to compensate by addressing his remarks to Kimmy. "You're sure? You'll hold my hand if I get scared?"

Kent moaned, but Kimmy grinned and held out her hand. "Promise."

Seb bit his lip, ignoring each stab of pain as he went through the process of pulling off his T-shirt, sitting himself up on the table and slowly lying down on his stomach. He had to laugh at the fact that the position put him practically nose to nose with Kimmy, who peered over the table edge close to his face with wide, encouraging eyes.

"You mind explaining it again before you hook me up to whatever this is?" he asked, mostly to buy himself time to recover from the painful effort of mounting the table. He wanted to turn and look at Kate as she worked behind him, but his strained muscles wouldn't let him twist his head that far.

"Nerves work on electrical impulses," she said in a clinical voice as he heard the snaps and clicks of something being assembled. "For some people," Kate continued, "we can interrupt the flow of pain sensation with another sensation. We teach the nerves to pass along this message instead of the pain message. Feel a tingle rather than pain. Often it works while the pads are on, but in some cases the nerves learn not to pass along the pain."

"I get it…sort of." Honestly, if it worked, Seb doubted he'd care if he ever understood how it worked. But still…electrical currents running through him? On purpose?

"If this works, this unit is portable enough you can use it while standing or walking."

"Then you'll really look like a toaster oven," Kent joked from his post off to the side.

"Very funny." Seb was surprised he was able to crack a joke. He was also surprised at how much he was hoping this worked. Even a temporary respite from the pain sounded wonderful. He feared he'd look like a walking lit-up Christmas tree with this gizmo on, but if it gave him relief and let him function, maybe it was worth it.

Kate walked into his view. "Before I put them on your back, I'll put a set here for a second so you know what it feels like." She gave him a long, powerful look that told him what she was going to ask next. He was ready—even eager—to comply. And so he couldn't help but give her a broad grin when she held out her palm and said, "Give me your hand."

Chapter Twelve

"Give me your hand." It felt like such a risky thing to say.

Kate had seen hundreds of bare arms, legs and chests in her work, but that hadn't prepared her for the sight of Seb's shirtless back. Of course, she reacted as any woman would to the attractive physique of a man like Seb. But that allure was cut with the sharp reality of the set of scars that ran across his shoulder blades and down either side of his spine. She'd never really asked him about the details of his motorcycle accident, and yet they shouted at her from the patchwork of scar tissue and wound lines that marred Seb's back. A battlefield of sorts—one where the war was still waging.

She was glad—in more ways than one—

that she'd chosen to bring Kimmy and Kent with her. The procedure and the small room felt far too close as it was.

"TENS can teach your neurons to stop sending pain signals. If it works, it will help you get back to work in the kitchen." Kate went through the procedure of attaching two electrodes to the back of Seb's hand.

"Stickers," Kimmy said, pointing to the white square patches.

"Very special stickers," Kate added, trying to stay clinical as she felt the warmth of Seb's hand—and his gaze. He was skeptical about the treatment—so were many of her clients. But she hoped Seb would join the dozens of them who had found genuine relief.

"Now we attach the wire," she explained, plugging the leads into the cell phone–sized control device. "And turn the system on. A very low level at first, just so you can get used to it. Ready?"

Seb said, "Yes," but didn't look like he totally meant it.

"Whoa," he said as the low hum of the device told her it was sending the signal. "It's... weird. It doesn't hurt, but it's...well, weird." He stared at the white patches delivering the odd sensation to the back of his palm.

"I tell my patients this simply talks louder than the pain so eventually your neurons change what they listen to."

Seb continued squinting at the white patches, moving his hand this way and that as if exploring what happened. "Okay, I get it." He tilted his head up toward Kate. "Fire 'em up."

"I hold your hand?" Kimmy said with adorable compassion.

"Kimmy," Kent moaned. "He doesn't need that."

Seb balked at Kent's disapproval. "Lemme tell you, kid, when a pretty lady asks if she can hold your hand, the answer is always 'yes.'"

Kate felt her cheeks heat up at the not-so-subtle reference to her recent request, not to mention the spark she felt whenever her hand touched Seb's. Chef Seb was the kind of man who could turn on the charm, even in considerable pain. They'd been so careful and cautious around each other, she wondered what would happen if he turned his charm on her full strength before the end of her time here. She hadn't met many men she would classify as irresistible, but Seb came frighteningly close.

It was a rather terrifying prospect to feel

that part of her slowly come to life again. Perhaps it was God's grace that it was with a man who held no prospects for a future life with her. The romantic version of the patches on the hand before the full healing of the patches on the back, she supposed, odd as the metaphor was.

Shaking off such philosophical thoughts, Kate peeled the small electrodes off Seb's hand and held up the sheet of four larger electrodes. "These go along your spine, and pack a slightly bigger punch."

"I've got a slightly bigger pain there," Seb agreed. "Put 'em to work."

Kate let the children engage Seb in chatter about silly topics—Franco the fountain frog and whether lunches had been any good without Seb in charge and who'd built the best birdhouse—as she affixed the electrodes and attached the set of leads. She smiled at how Seb made a big deal about how Kimmy held his hands. It sent her memory back to the warm moments back in the kitchen when he'd wrapped his hand around hers. It may have looked like thumb wrestling to the children, but it felt like a whole lot more between the two adults. She had to hold her hand over each of the patches for half a minute, pressing them down. It felt like a lot of touching—exactly what she'd been trying to avoid for most of her stay here. Now, every touch she gave to Seb's back felt charged— and not from the electrodes. The small control device now had four wires leading out of it, and she held it up in Seb's field of vision before she pressed the button to turn it on. "Here we go."

Seb jumped a bit as the electrodes delivered the gentle current. "Whoa," he said again, more in surprise than discomfort. "Still weird, only more." His face pinched as he tried to analyze what was happening. "So I can move now?"

She almost laughed. "No. It's not quite that immediate. You need to sit still at first and work your way up."

Kimmy gave Seb's hands a tiny, bossy squeeze. "Sit still."

"Can you turn it up or something?" he asked her.

"Not as much as you'd think—at first. You need to lie here for at least ten minutes while we slowly find out how high we can turn the current." She adjusted the controls. "How do you feel now?"

"Like a toaster oven," Seb said, shooting a look in Kent's direction.

Kate set the control box down. "Can you give me a more helpful description?"

"Mom," Kent cut in, "I'm hungry. Can I go see if there are snacks set out in the dining room?" There was always a counter with baskets of packaged chips, pretzels and other snacks on one side of the dining room. Seb had given Kimmy her own pink basket with safe snacks especially for her.

"Yes," Kate said. "That's fine with me."

"Hey, Kimmy," Seb said with a conspiratorial air, "I'm hungry, too. Will you go pick out some cookies for me?"

"Sure!" Kimmy said, without even looking to Kate for approval. She popped up next to her brother, who looked more than ready to leave the room.

"Be right back," Kent said.

"Take your time," Seb said.

Kate's stomach did a small flip at the savvy way Seb had maneuvered the privacy between them.

"Are you in any discomfort?" she asked, still using her clinical voice once her children left the room.

"I won't be if you sit down where I can see

you." He nodded toward the chair a few feet away from him at the head of the table.

Kate wouldn't admit to being afraid—well, maybe afraid wasn't really the right word; acutely aware, perhaps—of being alone with him. Even prone as he was, the man's swagger seemed to fill the room.

"I think it will help," he said with a sincerity she rarely heard from him. Did he know that soft voice of his was even more compelling than his usual bold declarations?

Seb waited until she was settled in the chair, then held her gaze for a long time. "Thank you."

"No one wants you to be in pain. This won't take it all away, but it stands a good chance of helping. And thank *you* for luring Kent back in the saddle, chili-wise." She'd forever be grateful for the way Seb found ways to pull Kent back out of his shell.

"Kate…"

A part of her kept coming unraveled when he said her name like that. She was grateful the kids could come back into the room at any moment. He rested his chin on his hands as if she were the most fascinating thing he'd seen in years. "You're beautiful."

Kate didn't know what to say. Was this

compliment a diversion? He seemed almost shocked that he'd said it out loud.

"That's a lovely thing to say to someone who's just made you hurt a lot." Not exactly witty, but she was thrown off guard by the look in his eyes. A dash of charm mixed in with a whole lot of anxious nerves.

"I kinda asked for it," he admitted. "But, well, you are. Is it okay to say that? I probably wouldn't in front of the kids, but…"

She gave him the only response that came to mind. "Thank you. And keep breathing until you're down to a five or so, pain-wise."

"I can handle more."

He was talking about the current, wasn't he? "Are you sure? We should take this very slowly." She was talking about the current, wasn't she?

"It's not pain. It's something, but it's not pain. I'd give anything to move without pain. Will these let me do that?"

She adjusted the controls up two points. "If it does work, you can wear this unit in the kitchen or walking around. But…"

He scowled. "But what?"

"But you'll need to be careful. You can't just slap these on and do everything. One spurt of pain-free activity and you'll probably go overboard and end up worse than when you started."

He gave a guilty smirk at how well she'd predicted his character. "Good thing I have you." Kate felt a zing of the nonmedical kind when he added, "You're supposed to be here on vacation, healing, and instead you're here trying to heal me. You're amazing, you know that?"

"And you're a little too generous with your compliments," she tried to tease, but fell short. Seb's attentions were hard to handle.

"Hey, I gotta lie here for ten minutes, and you're not the kind of person to leave a patient. I'm going to take advantage of a situation like that. And just in case you didn't know, those dimples ought to be illegal. On you and Kimmy both."

Kate fought the heat rising in her chest by reverting back to clinical mode. "I'll be counting on you to learn to use this wisely before I head back to Pennsylvania." She needed to remind both of them that her time here was short. "You won't have my supervision forever."

The room fell silent for a moment as they both considered that reality. "Kent's not the only one who needs to start over, Kate. You do, too. And believe me, the man who gets to heal that great big heart of yours had better realize the gift he's got." Kate didn't know what to make of the uncharacteristic resignation in Seb's voice at that bold statement. *It won't get to be me*, his tone said, even as his eyes told her he wished otherwise.

She was glad he realized it on his own, because she wasn't sure she had the strength to convince him.

The gizmo worked. Incredibly well. Seb had managed to cook one meal in the kitchen on Thursday and two on Friday. Now, on Saturday, Seb stood in the center of the dining hall, a circle of tables around him. Each family's chili entry was displayed proudly, and all the campers and staff were wandering among the tables, sampling and comparing.

He'd never tell Kate he'd behaved exactly how she'd predicted: overdone it with the TENS unit today and aggravated his back. He was counting the minutes until he could sit down and put the thing back on.

Mason walked up to him, grinning. "Glad to have you back in the kitchen. I don't think Dana and I filled in very well. If Rita from the Gingham Pocket in town hadn't shown up a couple of times, I think we'd have been sunk."

"You saying I have job security around here?" Seb needed to hear the answer a bit more than he was ready to admit.

Mason put a hand on his shoulder, forcing Seb to hide how it made a stab of pain run down his spine. "Always." The man nodded toward Kent, who was giving Dana a detailed explanation of his father's recipe—minus, of course, the secret ingredients, which Seb had vowed never to reveal as well. "Good job there. I was worried Kent wouldn't make it over that hurdle. Worried about both of you, actually." He gave Seb a serious look. "It wasn't your fault. In fact, it's because of you that it wasn't worse." He paused for a moment before adding, "Kent means a lot to you, doesn't he?"

Seb wasn't sure how much to admit. "I have a soft spot for him."

Mason raised an eyebrow. "Just him?"

"Kimmy's cute, too. Those dimples and those pigtails…"

Mason's resulting look told Seb he hadn't fooled his boss. He'd hoped he'd hidden his feelings for Kate, but evidently he hadn't. "I thought the hardest thing was getting ready for these families to come," Mason said wistfully. "Turns out it's harder to get ready for them to leave."

"Maybe it just means you're doing your job right," Seb offered, as much to himself as to Mason. "This place won't work if you don't care."

Mason nodded. "Makes me doubly glad for Dana. She evens me out. I even her out. And I think we'll sort of hold each other up between when one group goes and another comes." He looked around the room at the friendly competition between chili cookers and tasters. "These first families have been so special. Makes you wonder if any of the next ones will ever come close, you know?"

Seb had already realized no other family would ever come close to what the Hoyles meant to him. He stared at Kate as openly as he dared, feeling his heart ache as much as his back.

"She's leaving," Mason said quietly.

"I know," Seb replied. "That's how it's supposed to work."

"Doesn't make it easy."

No, sir, it doesn't. Still, no amount of lying to himself would let him believe he was what Kate needed. Seb knew he was a wild card, a whopping risk. Not—in other words—anything close to the man who could rebuild the life Kate Hoyle deserved.

The two of them stood together for a somber moment, taking in the happy activity swirling around them. With a sharp sense of irony, Seb realized that the camp to help grieving families just might need to help its chef work through his own sense of loss. *And your own sense of purpose*, he reminded himself. *This is just the beginning. You can let her go. It only feels like you can't.* Did they make TENS units for hearts? Could he find whatever current would block out that pain long enough to let him function?

"This is the most delicious chili you've ever tasted, right?" Kent boasted to Booker Domano with a confidence Seb had to admire.

"I dunno. Ours isn't so spicy," the boy replied. "This is crazy hot."

"That's what makes it good," Kent asserted, shoulders back and chin high. It had absolutely been the right thing to nudge him back into doing this again. Seb was grateful Kent would be going home well on his way to healing. He just couldn't yet be grateful Kent was going home.

Mason bumped his shoulder against Seb's, making Seb grit his teeth and hide a wince again. "You didn't stuff the ballot box or anything, did you?"

"I'd do no such thing," Seb balked with a dramatic air. "This is a free and fair election."

"Just checking," Mason said with a grin. "It's pretty obvious you have a favorite here." He checked his watch and announced to the room, "Voting closes in four minutes. Don't forget there's ice cream for dessert while we tabulate the votes."

"And nondairy pineapple whip for certain very special people," Seb added, looking straight at Kimmy. She returned his smile with a wide grin of her own. Those dimples. In fifteen years or so the boys wouldn't stand a chance.

"We're still having a campfire later, right, Mr. Mason?" Cindy Caldridge asked. "Ice cream is okay, but s'mores are way better." S'mores around the campfire had become a nightly tradition at the camp.

"I'd never deprive anyone of their chocolate," Mason teased. "Especially my future bride."

It was fun to watch how Mason's eyes still lit up like stars every time he referred to his future wife. *Give that to Kate*, Seb prayed. *And I'll need a little help dealing with the fact that it can't be me, if You don't mind.* He was going to selfishly bask in the glow of her presence as long as he could while she was here, but that would soon come to an end. It had to. Didn't it?

Seb watched as the final ballots made their way into a cardboard box at the end of the buffet table. Dana picked up the box, and she and Mason waved a temporary goodbye as they went off to Dana's office to tabulate the results.

"You heard the man. It's time for ice cream," Seb announced. He'd rounded up two of the men to help with the scooping since his back was no fan of the task. Declaring himself Master of the Toppings, Seb supervised the array of sprinkles, whipped cream, sauces, candies—but no nuts—and other goodies suitable for sundaes.

"Nothing like tryin' to get a boy to bed after a load of sugar," Devon Domano said to Seb with a wink. "Best load up on it myself."

"That's the tactic I suggest," Seb said with a laugh. It was going to be so much fun watching the smile on Kent's face as he accepted first place in the contest. It was going to be just as satisfying to watch the gleam of motherly pride brighten those irresistible dimples on Kate's face. Did he put an extra dollop of chocolate sauce on Kate's sundae? Maybe. Being Master of the Toppings should have a few advantages, and the load of kitchen pots and pans left after the day's cooking marathon was certainly daunting enough. He'd need that TENS machine for every minute he was allowed tomorrow. And a few ice packs, too.

"I haven't had this much fun in ages," Kate said, her eyes dancing. "I haven't eaten this much in ages. I won't need a s'more until next month, much less in the next few hours."

Seb let his eyes linger on hers. "When's the last time you indulged yourself? Just because it felt good and you deserved to have some fun?"

She caught his meaning, and the encouragement behind it. "Too long. Camp has helped me get better at it, though. It feels good to remember what fun is." As if to make her point, she topped her sundae with a cherry. She nodded over to Kimmy, sitting at a table with the Caldridge girls. "Thank you for making sure Kimmy could enjoy tonight, too. I was worried about the nuts."

"I told you we would keep her safe," he replied. "And I meant it. After all, her safety is part of why you can remember to have fun."

Seb wanted to save the sight of her smile deep in his memory. "And Kent. Tonight's going to be his night, you just watch."

Kate looked at Kent, clearing off his table with pride. "I'm worried he wants it too much. After all that business with those boys in town…"

"He's such a great kid," Seb said, not bothering to hide how much he liked Kent. "He's been through so much. It's going to make him a great man, you know. Strong. Full of heart. And I think the grouch factor will go away. Maybe not till college, though, so hang tight."

She laughed, and he tucked that sight away into his memory bank as well.

Dana and Mason returned to the room so quickly, it just enforced Seb's anticipation for an all-out Kent chili victory.

Which is why it hit him like a cannon through his chest when Mason announced the Domano boys as the winners, with a close second place going to Kent.

The disappointment in Kent's eyes sliced through Seb with a pain a mountain of ice would never touch. *What was I thinking? Why*

*did I set him up for this? What right did I have
to be so sure?*

Kent stood there for a moment, stunned,
all his pride and happiness folding in on itself like a crumpled leaf. "Kate," Seb said,
lost for what he could say to fix this.

The boy ran from the room, ignoring the
red second place ribbon Mason held out to
him.

"I did this. I'll go after him," Seb said, even
though he wasn't at all sure he could run fast
enough to catch up with the fleeing boy.

"No," Kate said. "No, don't." She set down
her ice cream, half finished, and dashed after
her son.

Seb watched Kate's indulgence of the
cherry slide down the slope of melting ice
cream. It settled, surrendered to failure, in
the bottom of the dish. *I didn't help at all*,
Seb thought with a bitter sense of regret. *I
just made it all worse.*

Chapter Thirteen

It had taken an hour to get Kent to talk about what had happened. It seemed like such a setback after so much progress. *It's my fault*, Kate thought to herself. *I should have seen this coming. Why did we ever think the contest was a good idea?*

At the end of an hour of trying, Kent was still not much more than a rolled-up ball of disappointment perched out of reach on his bunk. A knock came on the room door, and Kate opened it to find Mason.

"I'm sorry we let that happen," he said, pain and concern in his eyes. "There was no need for that to have been a competition. I hope you'll forgive our thoughtless mistake." He addressed the final remark to the top bunk, but no reply came.

Mason touched Kate's elbow. "Dana and the others are out by the fire with Kimmy. Why don't you let me have a chance to talk to Kent?"

"I don't know that he'll talk to you," Kate admitted. When Kent got in one of his moods like this, it was like talking to a stone.

"That's okay," Mason admitted. "I'm well acquainted with the silent sulk. It's okay if I do all the talking." He touched her arm again. "Go. We'll be okay. Try and get yourself a bit calmer while I take a stab at patching things up here."

She certainly hadn't gotten anywhere with Kent. Maybe someone else—someone who wasn't her or Seb—would have a better chance. "Okay." After a moment's thought, she added, "How is Seb?"

Mason nodded up toward the bunk again. "He locked himself in the kitchen, and I heard a lot of racket that sounded like angry dish washing, but I haven't seen him since. I'll give him a chance to cool off before I check on him." When the concern must have shown in her eyes, Mason added, "I suggest you do the same. Head to the fire, Kate. Kimmy's asking for you."

Other nights, the after-dinner gathering

around the fire was one of the best times at camp. Like every parent here, Kate appreciated the luxury of someone else doing the dishes and all the cleanup. The children of each of the families had formed a happy little group, the mix of older kids with younger ones creating built-in babysitting that let the adults relax by the fire.

Normally, it was wonderful for an exhausted single mother. Only, tonight had shown her how deeply tired she'd become. How had she not realized it? Had that exhaustion allowed her to grasp at unwise possibilities like the chili contest? To be so hungry for a win for Kent that she made a poor choice, or allowed others to? She was learning a lot about grief and loss here, but she was also learning a lot about how self-care was a wise choice to foster hope. She couldn't let herself get stretched so thin that she made wrong choices for her children.

Only, it wasn't only about stretching thin. It was about the things she was coming to feel. Her attraction to Seb had lured her into thinking new things were possible. Only, they weren't—not yet. Someday, yes, but not here and not now.

Despite the indigo sky and the warm eve-

ning breeze, so much of Kate remained un-
settled. Worry over Kent warred with a
worry over Seb she could not shake. Things
had gone deeply, horribly wrong tonight. It
felt like a whiplash against all the hope and
warmth she'd felt just…how long ago was it?
A mere three days ago? Time seemed tangled
tonight.

*What's the point of all this suffering? Where's
the healing we came here to find?* It felt like an
unfair thing to ask, a distrustful thing to say
to God. Especially when Kate realized she included Seb in that *we*. He was as set back in his
healing as she felt. As Kent now seemed to be.

She chose not to hide her anger and frustration from God. If she had learned one thing
in the months since Cameron's death, it was
that such things were best laid at the Lord's
feet without pretense. *He knows anyway*, Kate
always told herself when she came to God
with less-than-admirable feelings. *Better to
get it out so you can be healed.*

She walked over to Dana, who was standing on the far side of the glowing circle of
firelight. "This is all an awful mess," she said,
not bothering to hide her dismay.

"I know," Dana replied. "I'm worried. But
you should know that everyone gathered and

prayed before you came out here. For Kent, and Seb. For all of us, really. We're all still learning how to do this. But I'm trusting God's still at work, despite these great big bumps in the road."

"You won't ask him to leave on account of this, will you? He was just trying to help, trying to give Kent something he could feel proud of."

"Of course not," Dana said with a sigh. "We okayed the idea as much as he did. But he's taking it hard. You should have heard the clanging in that kitchen. He's mad at himself, and I expect his body is going to pay a price even that fancy device can't soothe."

"I agree." She lowered her voice. "I worry that leaving him in such pain is…risky." It felt dangerous to even speak the words.

"I don't understand a lot of it, but I think you're right. Still, so much of what would give him relief would only risk bigger problems. And the man has a rather legendary stubborn streak."

Kate was the only one of the camp families that knew of Seb's history of addiction. Most people—especially the women—had recognized the close friendship she and Seb shared, but no one knew the depth of it. "Stubborn may not prove to be enough. He's still in too much pain."

Dana's eyes told Kate she shared the same concern. "I'll admit that he needs to accept help. I was glad you got him to do that with the TENS unit." She sighed. "I'm just praying Seb remembers that we're all here for him right now."

Kate pulled Dana a bit away from the circle around the fire, lowering her voice. She dared to speak the thing that had been gnawing at her for the last hour. "I'm no specialist, but I worry this is a bigger battle than the first injury. Seb knows how the drugs can take away the pain. He knows the numbness he can hide in, how a relapse can stop him from feeling. That's got to be such a strong lure."

Dana's expression told Kate that the woman had been sharing the same concern. "I know. I've thought about that. But remember, Seb also knows what the drugs took from him. He knows what that rock bottom feels like. I like to think he'd fight to his last breath to keep from going back there. We've let him know how much we care about him. He needs to hear it, even if he says he doesn't want to listen." She gave Kate a knowing glance at that last statement.

Kate felt helpless to deny what she knew Dana was implying. "Yes." Even now, she silently sent a surge of strength to Seb and to Kent, along with a plea to God, to ease both their pains.

"Still," Dana said as if she heard Kate's thoughts, "it boils down to him, doesn't it? We can stand beside him—and we will—but we can't fight this for him."

Kate swallowed hard as Dana placed a hand softly on her arm. "I wouldn't count Seb out just yet. I think God's got big things planned for our chef. It's just going to be a long uphill climb to get there."

Kate looked back toward the circle of firelight, at the families that had already made such strides toward healing—her own included. "I can't think of a better place to do that climbing than here."

Dana smiled. "It means a lot to me to hear you say that. It's the kind of thing I wish Art Nicholson could hear. They're so busy being worried about what kind of people are coming here they forget they're actually people." She turned to Kate. "Would you be willing to meet him? Tell him your story? I can't guarantee it will be a pleasant conversation, but given all that's happened, I think you could have a big impact on him."

Kate balked. "After what his nephew did to Kent?" After all, she couldn't help thinking Nicholson's bully of a nephew was half the reason they'd gotten to this place.

"Maybe especially after what Tucker did to Kent. Look, I know I have no right to ask you to go toe-to-toe with Nicholson, but if you really think Camp True North Springs is worth fighting for, you're one of the best weapons we have right now. Will you think about it? For Kent and all the other Kents to come down the road?"

"I don't know that I'm strong enough to do something like that." She'd been in barely-scraping-by mode for so long she'd never considered herself capable of such a thing.

Dana turned to face Kate head-on. "Can I tell you what I see when I look at you?"

"Okay," Kate said, rather unsure what would follow a statement like that.

"I see a fierce fighter. A woman who doesn't give up no matter what. A woman who stares problems straight in the face, who tackles something enormous like Kimmy's allergies with courage even when she doesn't feel it. A woman who goes and finds the special equipment that can give our chef a shot at real relief. I'll tell you a secret. This camp doesn't heal you. It just gives you the space and grace to heal yourself. To let God do the work when you're open to it." She gave Kate's hand a strong squeeze. "That's what I see."

Kate felt her face flush in a way that had nothing to do with the heat of the fire. Dana was talking about some other woman, certainly not the shaking, doubtful, always-frightened person inside her own skin. "I don't know what to say."

"Say you'll take some of that fight and share it with those who need it. That's really the whole point of all this. Will you think about it?"

Her? Fight? For the camp and maybe for the person she'd become as a result of being here? It seemed like a good war to wage, even if she felt woefully inadequate to do so. After all, weren't such stretching places where God did His best work? "I'll think about it." Kate was proud of the tiny burst of confidence she was able to put in her voice.

Dana gave her a big smile. "Thank you." She cast her eyes out across the yards as if letting the camp know it had a new ally. "Well, now, will you look at that?" She pointed down the long drive that led from the buildings to the front gate. "Seb's come out of his room. Taking himself out for a walk to clear his head. He's going to come out of this and keep going. Kent'll see him doing it, too. That's got to be good, right?"

Kate followed Dana's gesture to the slow-moving figure of Seb walking down the drive. He walked like a beaten old man. If he really had taken his anger out on the dishes in the kitchen, he'd likely undone any of the healing they'd accomplished. She could almost guarantee he was in a lot of pain. Hurt, discouraged and exhausted.

Let him be. Trust he'll find his way back. Give that man over to God because you can't invest yourself like this in him.

She'd almost convinced herself to leave him be…until she looked toward the gate.

A large black vehicle was at the gate, lights off. Waiting.

The words came back to her like the blare of an alarm siren. *My good buddy with a full pharmacy in the back of his black van.*

No! Her whole soul seemed to cry out. *Don't!* Suddenly the warrior woman Dana described came roaring out of her. Without another word, she started walking down the drive after Seb, taking every ounce of her willpower not to break out in a run.

The driveway felt a thousand miles long, all downhill and into the darkest of valleys. Every single cell in his body seemed to be screaming at him, angry and hopeless. He couldn't spend his life hooked up to some device, and he couldn't feel past the pain when it wasn't on. He'd depend on it—or whatever came next—forever. Forever. There'd be no real healing, no going back to what he was. Invalid. Broken. Damaged. Just moving from mistake to mistake. He'd always known it, but somehow the reality of the relief—and it wasn't even full relief, just functional relief— took all the hope away.

It didn't make any sense, he knew that. But he was long past sense, and the thought of having to live the rest of his life like this, and without the support of Kate and Kimmy and Kent, felt desolate. Somewhere along the way he'd stopped being able to hope past the pain. It was just pain, everywhere, all around, every moment.

I can't. The two words kept dragging

him down the driveway, like a predator to the shiny black lair of Vic's van. *I thought I could, but I was wrong.*

He was sweating, gasping in short breaths by the time he fell up against the fence. He clutched at the metal links, wondering if he could stay upright long enough to do what he'd come to do. Maybe that didn't matter. Maybe nothing mattered.

"Seb!"

Kate's voice seemed to come to him from out of the dusk. And here he thought he couldn't hurt worse.

"Go away," he ground out through clenched teeth. *Don't be here. Not now.*

She came up beside him, breathless herself. She must have seen him and run after him. He should have waited until later. He should have done this in the dark of night like the awful thing it was. But the truth was he couldn't stand the pain one hour more.

"I will not go away." Her words had a defiance he'd never heard from her before. She grabbed his shoulder. "Don't be here. Don't do this."

"Who's your pretty friend?" Vic said, his voice smooth with amusement. Vic could afford to be charming. He already had what he wanted. What he'd been waiting for—for Seb's will to crack.

And crack it had. Crumbled, in fact. The only thing making it worse was that Kate was here to see it. What could be worse than that?

"Don't you come through this fence. Don't you set foot in here." Kate pulled up every inch of her tiny height, all mama bear ferocity against Vic. For him. Talk about your lost causes.

"That really ain't your call, sweetheart," Vic said with a syrupy sweetness. "My business is with Seb here."

"Go away, Kate," Seb implored, his whole body humming with pain and frustration now.

Kate didn't budge an inch. She turned to Vic. "I know who you are. I know why you're here. The man with the pharmacy in his black van looking for his best customer. Have I got it right?"

Why had he ever said anything to her? Why had he told her all about this? Why did he want her to care? It just made it all so much worse.

"I like her," Vic said, laughing in a way that made Seb's blood boil. "She's got fight."

"You steer clear of her," Seb warned. Vic didn't belong anywhere near the likes of someone like Kate. Vic came from the dark underbelly of the world, and Kate was all things good and sweet. Things he'd thought he could have in his life. Wrong. Broken people like him didn't get to have the Kates of this world on their side.

Suddenly Kate was pulling on his arm, trying to drag him away from the fence. "Come back, Seb. Just walk away with me. We'll figure it out." The pleading in her voice sliced through him—making his heart the only thing in the world right now that hurt worse than his body.

"I can't," he admitted, the two words feeling as if they pulled him down. "I can't."

"That's not true." She tugged again, and Seb prayed the ground would open up and swallow him. He didn't even have the will to pull out of her grasp. Her touch felt like the only thing holding him up, his last lifeline to the world he'd mistakenly believed could be his. "I know it's hard right now…" she went on, so excruciatingly kind.

"You *don't* know," he shot back, ashamed of his sharp tone. Seb tilted forward against the fence again, reaching into his pocket for the wad of cash. He hadn't even bothered to count it. There was no limit to what he'd pay to make the pain stop at this moment.

"Don't you take it. Don't you take his money. This has to be illegal. I'll call the police." Kate turned her face back to the camp and shouted, "Dana!"

Just when he thought it couldn't get worse. "Stay out of this," he growled, hating himself for being so mean to her. She didn't know. People like her could never know.

"Let's make this quick, Seb. I don't want to deal with that boss of yours." Vic held out his fingers through the fence links, stretching them for the cash. With his other hand Vic dangled a plastic bag Seb wanted to reach for with every cell in his body. *No pain. What did it matter if it came with no pain?* It would be worth anything to sink into the soft black nothingness again. It hurt too much to try and stay in the brightness, pretty as it was.

"No!" Seb watched in horror as Kate banged the fence so hard Vic yelped and drew his fingers back. She put herself between Seb and the fence, hands against Seb's chest. "Don't. Hang on. You can do this. *We* can do this."

Kate's eyes seemed like the only clear place left on earth. Tears wet her lashes, and her breath came in quick, frightened gulps. "Seb," she said. "Seb…" How had she known the thing that would pierce him most would be her saying his name like that?

"Just ten minutes. Give me ten minutes," she pleaded, tears coming down her cheeks. She grabbed his hand and folded it around hers, the way they had in that ridiculous thumb-wrestling match in the kitchen. He'd lost his heart to her in that silly moment. He wanted to raise their joined hands to his lips and kiss them, but he'd long since forfeited the right to do that—if he ever had it, which he didn't.

"I ain't got all day for this nonsense," Vic said, annoyed. "Call off your little friend here and let's do business."

Seb watched a circle of light from a flashlight land on the fence. "What's going on here?" It was Dana's voice. They would all laugh whenever she would occasionally use what Mason called her cop voice, and she was certainly using it now. Seb felt himself spiraling downward, the pain taking over everything else.

"I'm outta here," Vic said, stepping back from the fence. Seb felt as if the air left the world as the man receded. *That's it. I'm done.*

It's all over now. "Call me when you're on your own, Seb," he said as he rounded the front of the van. "I don't do spectators."

Seb heard Dana's footsteps crunching on the gravel behind him, her flashlight scanning the gate and the black van beyond it. Vic gunned the engine. "Who's there? Seb, who was that?"

"Nobody," Seb said, flat-out wanting to lie down and die. The ground was shifting under his feet and the edge of his vision was starting to turn black. "Nobody," he said again, although it seemed to take so much effort to get the word off his sluggish tongue.

"Seb, come on, Seb," came Kate's soft voice. It seemed so far away. So light and perfect next to his broken, heavy, aching self. "Come on back and we'll see it through." That's what she said, wasn't it? The words were starting to jumble inside his head.

The fence was cold and bumpy, every little edge jutting into his back as he slid down it. The ground really was swallowing him up. *Good.* It would all be better ended. Kate's sweet blue eyes were the last thing he saw before the black edges closed in and the pain pushed everything over the edge and into oblivion.

Chapter Fourteen

Save him.
  Guard him.
  Send him strength.
Kate couldn't think of any other prayer save those short, heartfelt bursts. She had no idea how to save Seb—only God knew that. She couldn't pray for his healing because she didn't know if Seb could be healed. She didn't know if she'd done the right thing in standing between Seb and his dealer. Maybe she'd only postponed the inevitable.

The only thing she knew for sure—which made her heart twist in fear and worry—was how much she wanted Seb to come back from this perilous edge. Back to her, and to Kent and Kimmy. The depth of that feeling scared her to her core. Seb Costa was a dangerous man to care for. He was a gigantic risk, and she had no place in her life for even the tiniest of risks right now.

Dana and Mason had all but dragged a nearly unconscious Seb back to his room after he'd collapsed against the gate. He'd been bathed in sweat and the most chilling emptiness filled his eyes whenever he managed to open them. He wasn't dead—he wasn't even really unconscious—but he was lost someplace no one could reach him.

She'd sat with him for the last hour. Rose and her girls had taken Kimmy and Kent without so much as a question. Kate was so shaken she didn't put up any resistance. She needed time to sort through her feelings as much as she felt compelled to stand guard over Seb.

She hadn't noticed until just now how sparse his living quarters were. Lots of the camp was filled with homey touches, with art and color and texture. She would have thought that someone with a personality as strong as Seb's would have a charismatic living space.

Not so. No art—except, she noticed with a pang, two drawings by Kent. No family photos like the one of Nonna that hung over the stove. The linens and curtains were functional, but not much more. It was the room of a man who wasn't sure he had the right to take up space in the world. That didn't seem like the man Seb was. Maybe he had been vibrant once, but he hadn't returned to that vibrancy yet.

Part of her could understand that colorless feeling, that echo-of-yourself existence. She wanted more for Seb—but that wasn't something you could give someone. That was something you had to give yourself. Life had certainly taught her that much lately.

They'd laid him facedown on his bed, following her instructions to cover his back with warm damp towels and a heating pad. Moist heat had the best chance of unlocking the steel cords of his tormented muscles. It was the only thing she could think of to do to reduce the sky-high level of pain she knew must be wracking his body.

He didn't seem to notice. She couldn't be certain at all that anything was helping. Eventually, she just sat in the chair next to the bed, closed her eyes and prayed. Really, what other true source of healing could she offer?

"You're still here?" Seb's worn-thin voice roused her from her prayers a while later.

All the spark and swagger were long gone from his features. He looked beaten and broken. In many ways, he was. Pushed to an edge she was grateful from which they'd been able to pull him back. "Yes," she replied simply. "How are you?"

He gave a half grunt, half growl that said more than any choice of words. Only, there was no strength in it. In fact, it sounded closer to a moan. Defeated. Humbled. A humble Seb Costa? It didn't suit him at all.

He lay so still. "Why?"

She planted her elbows on her knees to lower her face to meet his eyes. "Why?" Her sharp repeat of his question drew his eyes open again. "Did you really expect me to stand there while you threw your recovery away?" It surprised her how much she meant it.

He tried to turn toward her and halted in the attempt, wincing. "I blew my chance. Or would have. If you hadn't been there." His clenched fist told her the dependency of that was gnawing at him almost as much as the pain.

"Maybe that's why I'm here. In fact, maybe that's why *you're* here. Have you ever thought about that? That there would be a place for you among a bunch of people who need each other to get out from underneath their pain?"

He tried to shift away from her, but the pain held him still. "We're all weak and broken, Seb," she went on. "If there was some kind of pill I could take to make the pain of Cameron's loss go away, I can't say I wouldn't have drowned myself in them. I suppose plenty of people have found unhealthy ways to do just that. Lives fall apart in a hundred different ways. We need mercy. We need each other. We need God to fill in the places where we fall short. So we stand a chance of getting back up again."

She hadn't planned on making such a speech. She certainly wasn't qualified to preach to him—or anyone—on the virtues of suffering.

"I don't know that I can get back up again." The honest pain in his admission, the sheer desperation of it, pulled at her heart.

She reached for his hand, stunned by how tightly it was still clenched. "So don't, yet. Lay there and heal. Just don't think you have to do it all by yourself."

"Vic will come back. You'll be gone and he'll just wait until I fall down again."

There it was, the sharp and simple truth

that he needed her. Only, it was an equal truth that she couldn't be what he needed. Or perhaps it wasn't that she couldn't, more that she wouldn't. She could not put Kimmy and Kent through such a risk for more pain. She had to make choices that gave them what they needed—stability, dependability, people who would never let them down.

"You'll have Mason and Dana. They'll make sure you get other support, too. There's a group at the church in town Mason says you wouldn't join. I'd rethink that. You need it."

"And what if what I need is a feisty blue-eyed mama with more courage than sense?"

"No, Seb," she replied, with a certainty she didn't feel. She gave his hand one last tender touch before she made herself rise and walk toward the door. "I'm not what you need."

The next morning came hard, early and painfully. Seb had risen his first days at Camp True North Springs with a sense of purpose, shaky as it was. Today, he felt as if he was going through the motions. Existing rather than offering any kind of service. He took his time getting upright the way Kate had taught him, and then sat on the edge of the bed for a long time.

Kate. He couldn't pull his thoughts off her. "I'm not what you need," she'd said. Only, she was. She was like a life ring floating in a stormy sea—not the whole lifeboat designed to get him back to shore, but the first step in a long journey to safety. Whether she liked it or not—whether *he* liked it or not—he needed her.

But really, *was* she his path to safety? Hadn't last night shown him how far he was from safety? *It wasn't me who pulled me back. It was her.* He would have relapsed right then and there if Kate had not managed to pull him back in the nick of time. *I wouldn't have been able to do it on my own. I don't know that I ever will.*

His sense of failure was nearly swallowing him this morning. *I don't know where to go from here, Lord. I've failed You. I've failed Kate. I've failed Mason and Dana and the chance they took on me. And I have failed myself.*

Mason and Dana had expressed deep concerns—but mostly for his welfare. He'd fully expected them to let him go. After all, he'd proven himself undependable, hadn't he?

Only, they hadn't. Each of the people he cared most about had staunchly refused to let go of him, to leave him to the fate of his own faults. He was still here, still in recovery even if on shaky ground. But for how long?

What am I going to do?

The answer came to him in simple, solid words. *Put on the TENS unit, get yourself up and go do your job. Go serve. Go feed. Go on. It's all any of us can do.*

So that's what he did. He dragged himself to the shower and let the hot water ease his body back into some semblance of working order. He gave thanks for where he was—and where he wasn't—as he attached the unit to the base of his spine the way Kate had shown him. He turned it on and felt the singular buzzing sensation that stood between him and the pain. To call it relief was overstating it. But it was a welcome, bearable possibility. And today, that was enough.

Thank You, he prayed with each step that carried him to the big-house kitchen. *Help me*, he prayed as he put on the coffee and carefully reached for all the ingredients for chocolate chip pancakes. They were Kent's favorite. *Steady me*, he prayed as he set the large griddle onto the stove. *Be with Kent. Be with them all.* Maybe a handful of words, but more heartfelt words of prayer than he'd said in a long time. *Turns out You come to me anyways*, he told God, who failed to glower down on him in judgment as he'd expected. *Do You hear me no matter what?*

He normally worked with loud music, but this morning he served in silence. It seemed to fit the fragility of the moment. The quiet of a disrupted world waiting to see if it could keep going.

As he broke the multiple eggs into the bowl, it dawned on him: maybe he didn't have to be whole to feed them. He could do it broken. He'd been so intent on getting himself whole—thinking nothing else was possible until he did—that it never occurred to him he could work it out from here, right where he was. The man who would have walked out the camp gate to his own demise could still feed these amazing strong families healing so much better than he.

Kate was healing far better than he.

Well, that was the real problem, wasn't it? His weakness needed her strength. She made him believe in possibilities for himself. She had this way of anchoring him. He wanted her in his life. *I've always been great at wanting what I can't have, haven't I?* he thought to himself as he set the bacon into a frying pan and pulled out the pancake syrup.

Kimmy couldn't have a lot of things, but Kate had found ways to give her a pretty good life of happy work-arounds. Seb smiled as he got out the gluten-free pancake mix and egg substitute. There wasn't really a version of this for him because there was no substitute or happy work-around for Kate. She was either in his life or she wasn't. She was in his life for now, and he relished that, but the day was quickly coming when she would be gone.

I don't know who I'll be without her in my life, he thought as he set the batter into the mixer.

Normally, Seb would beat a problem into submission. He'd hammer away at something, throw himself against a challenge until he got what he wanted. Or, in some cases, became so battered that it no longer mattered. *That pigheaded stubbornness is probably the reason I'm still alive.*

Only, Kate wasn't like that. Kate wasn't a challenge to be conquered. She wasn't anything he could bend to his will. *Because I'm not what's best for her. Ugly truth, isn't it?* No, this was a sacrifice he'd need to lay down. She'd made that clear. *How do I find the strength to not fight for this? To let it slip through my fingers because I don't get to hold it?*

Seb had no idea. He could only hope that if he kept asking—pleading, actually—God would show him how.

"Hi."

Kent's tentative voice pulled Seb from his thoughts. The boy looked small and frail in the gray morning light. Needy. Unsteady. Pretty close to how Seb felt this morning.

"Hey, there." Seb stopped putting breakfast together and patted the stool by the counter in an invitation for the boy to sit. "I'm glad to see you." He really was. The urge to pull the little guy into a fierce hug rose up out of nowhere, but Seb tamped it down.

Kent climbed up onto the chair while Seb got out a glass of orange juice. "Rough patch, huh?" he asked the boy.

"Yeah."

Seb leaned both elbows on the counter. His back protested, but it was more important to be close to Kent. "I messed up," he admitted, his heart aching even more than his spine. "It shouldn't have ever been a contest."

Kent shrugged. "It woulda been cool to win."

"Maybe, but in order to have a winner,

somebody has to lose. Nobody should lose here. Your chili is awesome. I was hoping you'd let me use the recipe here at camp. After you're gone, I mean." The words caught thick in his throat. If he connected with families like this every session of camp, maybe he wasn't cut out for this sort of thing.

Kent looked up. "Can we call it Cameron's Chili? After Dad?"

Seb swallowed hard. "I think we should call it Cameron's Awesome Chili. Would that be okay?"

The smallest hint of a smile appeared on Kent's face. "Sure."

Okay. He'd put one small piece of life back into place. "Thanks," Seb said as he pushed himself up off the counter, wincing as he did.

"You hurt today?"

"Yeah, but not as bad as before." That was half true. Lots of him hurt worse than ever. "The gizmo helps." He held up a loaf of bread, eager to keep Kent's company with him this morning. "Want some toast?"

Kent nodded. As Seb put two slices in the toaster, the boy offered, "Mom's totally worried about you."

Seb just offered a grunt in reply, too worried any actual words would give away the sharp pang in his chest.

"Are you okay?" Kent asked.

That was the million-dollar question, wasn't it? After a moment's thought, the right answer came to him. "We're all sort of on our way to okay, but maybe not there yet. I think the whole point of this place is that it's okay here not to be okay."

Chapter Fifteen

Two days later, Kate fought the giant-sized lump in her throat. She was standing by the camp pond with all the other families. They were gathered next to a little bench that now held a basket of flowers. Blooms of all shapes, sizes and colors had been set there for a very special purpose—a purpose that now loomed large and painful. *I'm not sure I can do this.*

Dana had told her about the little ceremony that would take place toward the end of their stay here. It felt like the beginning of the end, the first steps in pulling themselves from the nurturing little bubble of Camp True North Springs and heading back out into the world. It sounded poignant and pretty when Dana described it, but Kate felt a mournful fear about the whole thing now that it was here.

Somehow this little ceremony had taken on the size of Cameron's memorial service— huge and full of sorrow—all over again. These weeks had brought so much back to the surface. Kate wasn't sure she could handle even this simple little ritual. And yet, she ought to, right? Surely this needed to be part of the healing process?

Her feelings must have shown on her face, because Dana came up to her. "Hey, you don't have to. If it feels like too much…"

Too much. How those words had echoed in her whole being so often the last few days. It was a change from the empty going through the motions that had kept her afloat almost two years, but the shift back into feeling was sharp and heavy. Light and healing in some ways, but still sharp and heavy in so many others.

Kent and Kimmy were already poking through the flower choices alongside the other children. The evening was a beautiful one, warm with a spectacular sky and just enough breeze to set ripples dancing across the surface of the pond.

"No," Kate said, pulling in a deep breath and straightening her shoulders. "I think I should try." She nodded toward her children.

"They seem to want to, anyway. If they can, then I should."

Mason stood at the edge of the pond in front of the gathered families. He held a bloom in his own hand. "My late wife was Hawaiian. She brought this ritual with her from her own heritage, teaching us how to remember those who were gone. In time, we used it to remember her." Mason's own tone took on the ache of loss that seemed to be Kate's constant companion. And yet he'd found a wonderful new life. She had to trust that was waiting out there for her somewhere in the future as well. It just had to be somewhere out there, not here.

"It's good to remember," Mason said, his voice catching just a bit. "Even when it's hard."

Kate let those words bolster her shaky spirit. *It's good to remember, even when it's hard. I want Kimmy and Kent to remember Cameron, always. I do, too.* Looking around, she could see that all the adults were wearing expressions of the same "I know this is important but it hurts" feeling that gripped her heart. She was in the company of companions. Fellow journeyers on the path of grief and healing.

Charlie stepped up beside his father, holding a large pink blossom in his hand. Kate took comfort from the strength in his young face. Children had a remarkable resiliency. She thanked God every day for the hope and inspiration Kent and Kimmy gave her. "Everybody gets a flower for everyone they want to remember," Charlie said with a touching importance. He held up the flower. "This one's for my mom. Here's how you do it."

As if it were that simple—which it absolutely did *not* feel at the moment—Charlie walked out onto the small dock-like platform that jutted just a few feet out into the shallow pond. He stood for a sweetly prayerful moment that tightened Kate's throat. Then, with an air of declaration, Charlie pronounced, "I remember Mom," and placed the flower gently into the water. He reached out and gave the bloom a little tap so that it made its way out toward the center of the pond.

He turned back to the small crowd. "Only, we have more than just Mom, and it's okay if you do, too." He walked back to the bench and gathered three other flowers. Everyone watched as Charlie went through the same process for three of his grandparents.

He'd lost so much. And yet she could see the healing in him. His sweet sincerity and the sadness in his words should have made

Kate want to cry—and there was no shortage of sniffles in the gathering at the sincere way he led the occasion. Still, there was an openness, a deep-breath quality in him that spoke powerfully to Kate and everyone else there. Mason looked touched and proud of his son, and for good reason.

They all stood for a moment, watching the slow dance of the four blooms as the breeze took them out into the water.

"You can do it whenever you're ready," Charlie said to the other children.

"We have more than enough flowers here for everyone," said a woman named Lorna, who said she ran the flower shop in town and donated the flowers as her way of supporting the camp. "Pick whichever flowers feel like your loved ones to you."

The two Caldridge girls went first. They each walked up to the basket and chose a red bloom. With strained voices and a set of small sniffles, the sisters held hands as they placed the pair of flowers out across the water in memory of their brother. Rose gripped her husband's hand as he cleared his throat.

There was a bit of a pause while everyone caught their breath, but then Booker and Brayton Domano walked up to the little dock and sent one white and one pink flower into the pond. Booker placed his carefully into the water in honor of his mother, but his brother chose to fling it while yelling, "We remember you, Mom!" Clearly, there was more than one way to partake of this remembrance, and it felt desperately good to feel a small smile steal its way into the somber moment.

The four Boswells went up together, both parents and the two boys, making them the first adults to take part. Each of them held yellow flowers, which had been part of the university colors of the campus where their son and brother had been killed. Ron, Heidi and their two boys quietly said, "We will never forget you, Doug," as they laid the flowers in the water to join the others. There were several blooms in the water now, and they circled each other and spread out in a colorful arc. A flotilla of beauty on the breeze, making its way toward the center of the pond.

It was just them, now. Kent looked at her, and Kate felt the unsteadiness return. Could she really do this? It seemed so simple and so enormous at the same time. She took a deep breath, hoping it would help, but still felt stuck in place.

Kimmy tugged on her hand. "Mama, I want a blue one."

"Sure, honey," she replied, only she still couldn't make her feet move toward the basket of flowers.

Dana offered a supportive glance, and suddenly Kate felt as if every eye was on her. It was Kent who stepped in. "C'mon, Kimmy, I'll help you."

Kate fought tears and a startling paralysis as Kent led Kimmy up to the table. He not only helped her with a blue flower, but chose a blue one of his own. *In so many ways he's stronger than me*, Kate cried in her heart as a tear stole down her cheek. *I don't think I can do this. This is silly. Why can't I?*

"Go on." Seb's voice came softly from behind her. She hadn't heard him come up. She felt his hand gently touch her shoulder. "You can do this."

"I can't," she almost whimpered, ashamed of herself.

"Yeah, you can," he said, his voice warm and reassuring. "You're strong enough, and I think it'll help."

She'd said something very similar to him while he complained of how much his exercises hurt. She couldn't very well go back on her own advice, now, could she?

She turned to look at Seb, stunned by the sad compassion in his eyes. He knew all about pushing through pain. Pain of all kinds. He knew what it was like to feel like "not enough." He nodded at her, a million unspoken words playing across his features.

The first step toward the flowers felt enormous. But the second felt smaller, and before she knew it, she was picking up a purple bloom that looked a lot like the flowers she'd carried in her wedding bouquet. And while the memory was sharp, she was surprised to discover it was also sweet.

"We remember Dad." Kent's voice broke a bit as he set the flower in the water.

He held on to his sister's waist—tight and possessive—as she squatted down and said, "For Daddy," and used both hands to toss a big blue bloom into the pond.

She walked up behind them, placed the purple flower in the water and said "Cameron" softly as she tapped it, sending it out to float beside the blooms her children had launched.

What everyone said was true. Something broke free in her chest as she set the flower out on its memorial journey. Something settled, a hole still there, but somehow with less jagged edges. As if her soul took a deep breath. She felt the breathing of all the grieving families, as if they held each other up like the water held up the collection of flowers traveling together out into the water.

Kate felt just enough grace to be able to offer thanks. *This is a good place, a healing place. Thank You, Lord, for bringing me here.*

Seb stood on the edge of the gathering, not wanting to intrude on the tender moment. He'd stepped in just enough to nudge Kate, but that was all he should do here. This was a time for the families, part of the mission of Camp True North Springs.

In truth, he'd found the idea of sending the flowers out across the water a bit silly when Mason told him about it. It would be part of every family's stay here, they said. He'd kept his skepticism to himself, seeing as Mason and Dana knew more about this sort of thing than he did, and they signed his paycheck, after all.

Now, having watched the simple little ritual, he got it. He saw the changes in the faces of the families as they sent their remembrance flowers out into the pond. Something broke open in everyone—even Charlie and

Mason—and it made space for more healing. There was a huge power in that, even if he didn't fully understand it. Seb stood there for a long time after the families and Mason, Dana and Lorna went back into the big house for some refreshments he'd already set out.

He found he couldn't leave. He stood there, trying to unpack what he'd just seen and how deeply it had sunk into his own spirit. This wasn't for him, and yet somehow it felt like it was.

There were a few flowers left in the basket Lorna had left on the bench. He kept staring at them, at a loss to understand why he felt drawn to the blooms. *I've not lost anyone. This isn't for me. I'm just here to help it happen, not to get involved.*

And yet, the sense of his own losses seemed to surround him. His body would never be as strong and capable as it once was. This week had shown him his life would never be without the constant watch of recovery. The vigilance, the struggles, those would always be with him.

And Kate would not.

He'd seen how Heidi Boswell clung to her husband as they bore their grief together. He'd seen Kate watch them, too. It wasn't hard to know she must feel a longing to not have to do this alone. A falling apart or just-falling-together life must be easier with someone to lean on. He'd felt it himself, made strides and surmounted obstacles easier these weeks because of Kate. He hoped—no, he prayed—he'd been just the smallest bit of help to her.

But the end of the week was coming. And with it, Kate would be going. Kate should go. She had a life back in Pennsylvania, and the kids had friends and school and lives far beyond a tiny camp on an Arizona mountainside.

Kate had to be just a passing season in his life. In a few days she would be a memory. A very pleasant, very tender memory.

It hadn't really dawned on him until this moment that he was grieving, too. He'd been spending so much energy fighting and clutching that it never occurred to him that perhaps the way forward was to let go. Did he have it in him? It seemed as if only a much stronger man could pull off something like that.

He didn't deserve a bloom. But could he respond to the urge to send something out into the water, to reach for the healing this little ceremony seemed to offer? He couldn't deny it.

Seb looked around, making sure no one was watching. With care, he selected a beautiful large lush green leaf and two smaller ones. Feeling as compelled as he did ridiculous, he walked to the end of the little dock and squatted down. The small act of placing the trio of bright green leaves into the water felt huge. He made sure they faced up so they could float, and with a tiny tap he sent them off across the ripples to catch up to the other blooms.

"I will remember her," he said quietly, but still recognized it was something that needed to be said out loud. "And the kids," he added, managing a smile. "And I'll try to stay grateful You sent them into my life." That felt like a whopping promise to make God given the way he felt at the moment, but it also needed to be said.

He stayed there watching the leaves slowly slide across the water for a long time. The setting sun, drawing shadows across the pond so that eventually it was hard to see the distant flowers, seemed to suit the moment. It had cost him a lot to hunch down and reach into the water, and the aches in his muscles told him he couldn't stay. His back complained loudly as he slowly worked his way upright.

But somehow, it felt as if he walked a little taller as he made his way back to the kitchen.

Chapter Sixteen

"Please understand, it's not personal." Arthur Nicholson was doing an excellent job of looking down his nose at Kate as they stood talking on the North Springs Community Church lawn Thursday afternoon. The camp families were here at the church for a send-off afternoon picnic as they wound down their time in North Springs. The event was pleasant. Her current conversation, not so much.

Kate wanted to do all she could to support the camp. And Dana was right—her story in particular, given what had happened with Tucker and Kent, might persuade Arthur. Still, every minute spent talking to Arthur Nicholson was convincing her there'd be no changing this man's mind. Ever. Kate didn't see how anything she could say to him would budge his disdain.

"I disagree," she said, putting as much confidence as she dared into her voice. "This must be something that everyone takes personally. We're not statistics or demographics. You can't cast us as stereotypes. We're families."

"You can't tell me that poor choices didn't place some of these kids in the spots they are. Surely you understand our reluctance to play host to that."

Poor choices? What poor choice did Cameron make in trying to get home early to his family? Why should a shortcut take a man's life?

"The only person who made a choice to bring this tragedy upon our family was a stranger holding a gun who wanted to steal Cameron's car."

That stopped Nicholson for a moment, and with a burst of surprising bravery, Kate added, "I'm not sure I could say the same of your nephew. Roughing Kent up and calling him 'one of those camp boys'?" She held the man's gaze with her most protective mama-bear glare. "I'd call *that* a poor choice. Where do you suppose he got the idea to think of the camp families—of *us*—like that?" If this was the last time she got to speak to Nicholson, she was going to make sure he had no doubt how she felt.

"The residents of this town have a right to protect what's theirs. Did Mason tell you what a battle it was to get approval to even set up the camp in the first place?"

"I did," came Seb's voice from behind her. "Not one of our town's finer moments, if you ask me."

"I don't remember asking your opinion." Nicholson scowled. It was clear these two men had a history—and not a pleasant one at that.

"I really like North Springs," Seb said. "The people here have been very good to me. Well, *most* of them." Seb left little doubt who he meant by "most."

"Our town has done a great job of welcoming the rehab center residents, even when it's been difficult. I think that should be enough." There was no doubt who Nicholson meant by his statement, either.

"You've *tolerated* some of us well enough." Seb emphasized the word. "I'll give you that. But I think North Springs has enough heart for both organizations. This church may be the first church some of these families have ever known. Have you thought about that?"

"Exactly what are you getting at?" Nicholson challenged.

A fight was not the point of this afternoon. This picnic was supposed to be another chance for the town and the camp families to meet each other. To see each other as people. To lay the groundwork of hospitality and cooperation for all the Camp True North Springs families that would come after them.

Kate stepped between the two men with one last effort. "I came here to have a conversation, Mr. Nicholson, not an argument."

"My nephew could tell you how good Costa is at starting arguments."

Seb's eyebrows furrowed down. "I could say a lot about who started what, Nicholson. I wouldn't have had to step in and rough Tucker up if he wasn't already shoving her son against the wall."

"Both of you, stop," Kate commanded. She didn't have the strength to be playing referee right now. "I think we can all agree this conversation is over." She grabbed Seb's elbow and began leading him away from Arthur Nicholson's irked frown.

"No, it's not," Seb tossed back as he let Kate lead him away.

"Oh, I think it was over before it started,"

Nicholson replied, in an infuriatingly superior tone.

Dana and Mason had heard the raised voices and were making a beeline over to Kate and Seb. "I'm sorry I ever suggested this," Dana apologized. "I really thought meeting you would help change his mind."

"I tried," Kate admitted. "But he's such an unpleasant man."

"He's in the minority," Mason said, blowing out a frustrated breath. "He's just very loud about it."

Dana touched Kate's arm. "More and more of the town is coming to see how much good the camp does. Look at what's happening here—all the conversations happening between camp families and church families. Maybe it's just a lost cause to try and bring Arthur around. Our welcome has always been here, not the town zoning board."

The sound of carefree childhood laughter did indeed fill the afternoon air. Food and games had made for a delightful time on the church lawn. Kate had found the church services here to be heartfelt and heartwarming. Church at home was a lovely, supportive place, but Kate had to admit there was something so healing about being somewhere

where people didn't constantly look on her as "that poor woman."

Several people had asked her why she chose to stay in Pennsylvania, not make a fresh start somewhere else. These weeks were making her pose that same question to herself. Only, somewhere else kept looking very much like here. She was feeling a pull to this mountainside that had nothing to do with just a vacation. Trouble was, she knew too much of that pull had to do with the man beside her.

I've got to trust my head over my heart right now. The true north the camp sought to give her felt far away, and her bearings felt murky and unrecognizable. This was no time to make life-altering decisions.

"Mom!" Kent's shout of alarm yanked Kate out of her thoughts. He was running toward her with Kimmy's backpack, pointing to his sister gathered in Tina Caldridge's arms.

Even from here, Kate could see the puffing in Kimmy's eyes and face. "Kimmy!" she yelled, running toward her daughter even as the child began coughing and wheezing.

Kent unzipped the backpack and thrust the EpiPen pack into Kate's hands. "Call an ambulance!" she yelled to Dana and Mason behind her as she unwrapped it and pulled the cap off the syringe. Kimmy tried to scream—the poor dear knew what was coming—but couldn't pull enough air in to make any sound. Kate fell to the ground, trapping a squirming Kimmy's arms and legs with her own. With the precision of someone who'd done it too many times, Kate positioned the needle over her daughter's thigh and hit the activating button to send the life-saving injection into Kimmy.

Seb was behind her, holding her shoulders steady.

Kent was beside her, his voice frantic. "Is she okay?"

"Your mom knows what she's doing. It's gonna be all right," Seb said to Kent.

"Breathe, honey," Kate said in as steady a tone as she could manage. "Let the medicine work, and breathe. Seb's right, it'll be okay. Just like the other times." She stroked Kimmy's puffy and blotchy cheek, trying not to let the girl's frightened whimpers slice at her heart. Now was the time to act—she could get scared later.

"Mom, is she *okay*?" Kent asked, kneeling down to grab Kate's arm.

Kimmy coughed and erupted into an anguished cry. It was a good sound—it meant her airways had expanded enough to let her get in enough breath to cry. "She will be. She will be."

"What happened?" Dana asked Tina as Kate began gathering up everything and the sound of a siren came closer.

"She got a hold of a peanut butter cookie somehow," Tina said. "I don't know how. We were all being so careful. We told everyone."

"I didn't watch her," Kent nearly wailed. "I shoulda watched her." He took his guardianship over Kimmy so seriously—it was too much weight for a boy his age.

I should have been the one watching her. I let my guard down. She's only three. She can't defend herself against these kinds of things. Kate's heart felt as if it were falling to dust. Only, it couldn't now. She couldn't go to pieces now. There would be time for that later but not now. "It'll be okay," she said to both her children, even though nothing felt farther from the truth. "Let's let the doctors look her over and then it'll all be okay."

"Kate..." Seb was helping the two of them up. He looked positively stricken. She knew, in that moment, how much he cared about little Kimmy. About all of them. Yes, he'd probably never seen the particular drama of thrusting a syringe into a choking child. She'd done it dozens of times and it still chilled her to the core every time. But it was more than that.

Do what needs doing, she told herself, clutching Kimmy to her chest and pushing past the fear to be grateful for each wheezing breath she heard from Kimmy's lungs. *Get her to the hospital*. This was a close call, one that reminded Kate that there might come a time when it wasn't close at all…

"Is she gonna be okay?" Kent had repeated that question to Seb a dozen times as they drove toward the medical center behind the ambulance.

Seb didn't know what to say. What did you promise a child in a situation like this? And that was it—for all his seriousness and responsibility, Kent was a child. Ten years old, for crying out loud. What ten-year-old should be expected to shoulder burdens like this? "She's been okay all the other times, right?" It was a rather pathetic response, but nothing else came to mind.

"I suppose." Doubt dragged the little guy's words down. He sank even farther into the back seat of Seb's car in a way that made Seb's heart ache.

"She's got your mom, and the paramedic guys, and everyone at the hospital." He tried to think of something—anything—to encourage Kent. "And you got to her medicine right away. She's blessed to have you looking out for her the way you do."

He wasn't good at this sort of thing. He was usually the guy *causing* the crisis, not the one trying to solve it. But since the paramedics had only let Kate in the ambulance with Kimmy, and Kent had rejected Dana and Mason's attempt to drive him to the hospital in favor of riding with Seb, here he was. Truth be told, he was glad to do it. It made him jittery to just sit there and watch the panic unfold. The powerful protective streak this family had sprung up in him would not be denied. If it meant driving Kent all the way to Flagstaff instead of the fifteen minutes to the local medical center, he'd have done it.

Kent's worried silence seemed to fill the car. "I mean it, kid," Seb went on. "You do a great job of taking care of Kimmy." A disturbing thought struck him. "You're not thinking any of this was your fault, are you?"

Kent seemed to sink down even lower in the seat. Dana had told him Kent was too small to safely ride in the front seat, and he got that, but it seemed as if the boy was a thousand miles away all the way in the back.

"'Cause it absolutely was not," Seb declared with all the authority he could put into his voice. "This was one person not understanding what Kimmy couldn't have. This wasn't about your keeping watch, or your mom keeping watch, or even me." That didn't stop the icy finger of guilt that kept creeping up Seb's spine. He'd promised Kimmy would be safe while she was here at the camp. He was in charge of food. He had researched and knew all of Kimmy's requirements. He should have talked with the picnic coordinators at the church so that they understood how strict things had to be. Maybe even taken on the food prep himself. Kate should have been able to trust he was taking care of that. Have confidence in his protection so she could grab a tiny sliver of peace and healing.

It seemed forever until they turned the corner into the ER parking lot. Seb pulled into the visitor's spaces while the ambulance swung under the portico with lights flashing. A squad of hospital folks in scrubs scurried to meet Kate and Kimmy. Everybody looked very intense, but nobody looked like disaster would strike at any moment. This was, hopefully, just a close call. *Please, God, let it just be a scare. Nothing more.*

Even if it was only a close call, it would be one of hundreds Kimmy might endure in her lifetime. The weight of that pressed Seb as deeply into the car seat as Kent seemed to sink. This thing was relentless. Way too many things in his life felt relentless right now, demanding a nonstop vigilance he didn't seem to have the strength to endure.

He managed to reach Kent's hand just as the boy was trying to scramble out of the back seat. "Whoa, there. Don't go flying out into the parking lot and make everything worse." He gave Kent a steady gaze. "We're gonna do our best to walk into there calm, okay? Can you do that for your mom?"

"Okay." Kent's nerves were strung tight, and with good reason. No ten-year-old should be this familiar with emergencies. With tragedies. It struck Seb with a new fresh pain that the boy was in dire need of stability. Dependability. The very things he could never promise Kate and her family.

But there was one thing he could do: he could get them through today. Or at least help. His muscles were starting to complain at all the activity, and the TENS unit only had a fraction of its charge left. Ignoring that, Seb straightened his spine to something he hoped looked like strength as he got out of the car. He came around to where Kent was obediently waiting by the side of the car and reached out his hand to the boy.

Something sweet and sharp took over his heart when Kent placed his hand in his and gripped it tight. He gave Kent's hand a reassuring squeeze. "It's gonna be okay. You knew what to do, your mom knew what to do and everybody in there knows what to do. Plus, I expect you've got a whole army of church folks sending up loads of prayers. So let's try not to worry, okay?"

Kent just nodded. Seb wanted to pull the boy into a big, tight hug, but feared it might be the wrong thing to do. Kent was already too attached to him—his insistence at being driven by Seb had shown that. This needed to be handled carefully. He needed to stay on the edges of this family no matter how much his chest ached at the thought.

Seb's breath hitched as they walked through the sliding doors of the emergency room. He'd forgotten how the atmosphere of an ER took him to dark places. Out of nowhere, his mind brought back the bouts of blinding pain, the fog of the pain pills, the particular panic of being all alone in a crisis. *No one ever held my hand into the ER*, he thought, doubling his grip on Kent's small fingers. No way was he going to let Kate or Kent—or even Kimmy— go through this without someone watching out for them.

"Kate and Kimmy Hoyle?" he asked the nurse at the receiving station.

"Are you family?" she inquired.

"I'm not, but he is," Seb replied, feeling that sting for a bit.

"She's my sister," Kent piped up, in a panicked voice.

That brought a smile from the nurse. "I hear you were quite the hero today. Good job getting her to your mom quick like that." She looked up at Seb. "Take him down to bay four, and then I'll need you to hang out here while they finish the assessment. She'll need some more meds, and most likely we'll keep her overnight for observation." She pointed in the direction of a wing of curtained alcoves. Seb didn't even need the numbers painted above each one; he could hear Kimmy's cry and the murmur of Kate's calming voice.

Kimmy looked so small on the large hospital bed. All the charming brightness of the little girl's eyes was lost behind frightened tears. Blotches filled her puffy face and lips, and he noticed that a bandage—from another shot?—sat on her thigh. It seemed all kinds of wrong to have all that going on to such a small child.

"You're gonna be okay, Kimmy," Kent said bravely as he slid his hand from Seb's grasp to walk over and take his sister's hand. The act struck Seb as an all-too-accurate picture of how things had to go from here.

"Seb," Kate said, her eyes conveying a heart-wrenching mixture of fear, gratitude and relief. She gave Seb's hand a quick squeeze of thanks while not letting go of Kimmy's. Again, the gesture went through Seb's heart before he could stop it. "Thank you," she said, then said thank you again as if once wasn't enough.

He'd helped. Seb tucked that into a corner of his heart and held on to her words and the look in her eyes. It didn't seem nearly enough, but it was something. Life had taught him that sometimes you just take what you can get and do what you can do, whether it makes the grade or not. Some people got golden lives, got everything they wanted, waltzed through life with success and influence.

Others didn't. He'd been given the chance

to lighten the load for the three people in front of him, even for just a little while. He should try and be grateful for that and not crave more.

But as he turned to walk back to the waiting room, Seb knew he probably wouldn't succeed.

Chapter Seventeen

"Can I go tell Seb they moved us up to a room?" Kent asked as they settled Kimmy into the pediatric wing where she'd stay the night.

Seb had stayed in the waiting room for the hours it took to process Kimmy through the ER. These things were never quick, and everyone was weary. Kate was glad Kimmy finally had nodded off, exhausted from the trauma of her allergic reaction despite the multiple steroids and inhalants that could often make her jumpy. She herself was experiencing that particular blend of alertness coupled with weariness that accompanied any such crisis. And it was always so much harder alone.

Of course, she wasn't truly alone—she had Kent. And then there was Seb's distant presence, a distance she knew he was keeping on purpose. She'd have to figure out what to do about that, but not right now. Right now, dealing with it simply meant allowing Kent the several trips he'd requested back and forth from the ER bay to update Seb. She wasn't sure it was especially wise to let Kent wander around even the small medical center alone, but Kent seemed to need Seb in the picture. He took comfort in knowing that the man hadn't left. If she was honest, so did she. "Okay." After a moment's thought, she added, "And you can ask him to come up if you like."

Kent had asked, actually, several times from the ER bay once Kate gave her permission to the nurses. But despite making several runs to the vending machines for snacks and such, Seb had stayed in the medical center lobby.

Kate could guess he'd continue to refuse—it was smart, after all, to keep his distance on account of how raw everyone's feelings were. Still, part of her longed to borrow his bravado, to feel like she wasn't holding everything up on her own. She was worn thin, and if Seb walked into this room right now and showed even the smallest hint of compassion, she might puddle right into his arms.

And that was not what was best. Still, she couldn't have Kent shuttling back and forth the longer distance from the pediatric ward to the hospital lobby. Besides, visiting hours would soon be over so even if Kent did convince Seb to come up, it wouldn't be for long. Maybe she could manage a short visit.

Because after that would come the long night of snatching bits of sleep with Kent on the hard vinyl couch under the windows in Kimmy's room. She'd done this before. She knew better than trying to convince Kent to go back to camp with Seb—her son would not leave his sister. *He bears too much for her*, she thought. *It's not fair.*

Kent returned ten minutes later without Seb, but with a tote bag. "Chef Seb had Ms. Dana and Mr. Mason bring this over," he said. "There's sweatshirts and some food and my book and stuff."

Kate attempted a smile. "That's very kind of them. I hope you said thank you."

"I did."

"Chef Seb didn't want to come up?"

She didn't know what to do with the disappointment in Kent's eyes as he shook his head. The adults knew there needed to be boundaries drawn here, but that didn't mean

Kent understood why. She'd find a way to thank Seb later for showing the resistance she felt incapable of at the moment.

The couch vinyl squeaked as Kent plunked himself and the bag down. "Are we gonna have to go home after this? When Kimmy's okay, I mean?"

Their car was still at the church, but she'd find a way to get them back to camp in the morning. "We don't know yet, honey."

"I don't want to go back."

She looked at Kent. "Surely you don't want to stay in the hospital any longer than we have to."

"No, I mean, are we going to have to go *home*? To Pennsylvania. I don't want to."

Kate wasn't expecting that. "Why? Your friends are there. You'll start fifth grade this year—you were excited for that."

"I like it here." His words had such a soft tone, as if he were apologizing.

With everything that had happened? Tucker Nicholson's treatment of him and the day they'd just had? Kate balked for a moment, until she recalled the transformation that had begun to take place in Kent—before every-thing went wrong, that is. She'd been trying very hard not to permit the same feeling rising up in her. *I like it here, too. I just can't see how it would work. I'm not even sure it's real—just a temporary illusion.* Camp True North Springs wasn't real life. All the stress and friction of an everyday existence would only be held at bay for a short vacation. Then real life would grow up all around it no matter where they were. The last few hours had taught her that, hadn't they?

She sat down next to Kent. She tried to find a way to help the boy sort through his experience. "It does feel different here, doesn't it?"

"Nobody looks at me funny here. And Charlie's nice, even if Tucker is a doofus."

Kate managed a quiet laugh, thinking she knew some people with harsher names for Arthur Nicholson and his nephew than doofus. But Kent had a point—the scuffle he'd had with Tucker would have derailed him for weeks back in Pennsylvania. He seemed stronger now. She treasured the hope that gave her. It reassured her that Kent would fully heal—not forget, but fully heal—from this whole dark season.

But any mother can read her son, and Kate saw what Kent was thinking—it was all over his face. "You like Seb, too."

"He's awesome."

Kate smiled at how much Seb would enjoy that endorsement. "I think he's the perfect chef for a place like Camp True North Springs, don't you?"

Kent shifted to face her. They paused for a moment while Kimmy made a small noise and shifted in her sleep. The room seemed close and quiet in the soft glow of all the monitors and the low light of a single fluorescent tube over Kimmy's bed. For all this medical center's attempt at homey touches, a hospital still looked and felt and smelled like a hospital.

"He was really worried about Kimmy," Kent offered. "And you. He asks me all kinds of questions about you. And he stares at you. A lot." Kent leaned in. "He told me he thought your dimples were even cuter than Kimmy's." After a small pause that made Kate gulp, he scrunched up his face and asked, "Are you guys allowed to like each other like that?"

Kate almost had to cover her mouth at the burst of laughter that threatened to come after a bombshell like that. *The things kids notice when we don't think they're watching.* And to Kent's credit, it was a whopper of a question. She gave the only answer that came to mind. "It's complicated with grown-ups."

Kent rolled his eyes. "Seb said the same thing when I asked him."

Kate bolted upright. "You *asked* him if he was allowed to like me?" Embarrassment and amusement battled each other in the pit of her stomach.

"Well, no. I said it differently. He didn't answer. But he got a funny look on his face for a long time after that."

I can only imagine, Kate thought.

"I think that's why he wouldn't come up. I mean, he wants to. I can tell. I don't get what's going on. We're all happier here. Jimmy's family moved after his grandpa died. Can't we move here? Is there some rule I don't know about?"

She struggled for a way to explain the complexity of it all to her son. "All of us—you, me, Kimmy, Seb—we have things to work out. Big things. I'm not so sure we can mix all of that up." Oversimplified, perhaps, but pretty accurate for the circumstances.

Kent's eyebrows furrowed even deeper. "I don't get it. Doesn't everyone say the whole point of camp is so that families with big things to get over can do it together? So it's not true for us? 'Cause I feel like it is."

It was mighty unsettling to get such a challenge to her thinking from her own ten-year-old. Were it not so alarmingly true, it might even be funny. If the whole point of Camp True North Springs was to heal together, why was she so insistent they heal apart?

The answer struck right to the core of Kate's deepest fears. She could never be certain that the care she'd come to feel for Seb could carry them through their mutual brokenness. She needed stability, and he didn't have it. And Seb needed more grace than she felt capable of extending him. It was as if they were each not even half a person, so they had no hope of coming together as a whole.

It was too much uncertainty, too much to risk.

Wasn't it?

What if less-than-half and less-than-half made more than a whole? What if that coming together was how less-than became more-than-enough?

Her heart suddenly ached so fiercely in the face of Kent's challenge that she was afraid to speak. She couldn't come up with any words. If she did, Kate feared all the pent-up emotion would come gushing out of her and confuse Kent further.

It wasn't as simple as he thought. It couldn't

be. She'd been thrust into an endlessly complicated life the night Cameron died, and that was simply a fact that must be faced, even if Kent couldn't see it right now.

Kent gave her a glare that reminded her so much of Cameron it sent a shiver down her spine. The kind of old-soul, too-serious glare of which no ten-year-old should be capable. As if he knew better than she. "He should be up here, Mom. He shouldn't have to wait in the lobby."

Desperate for some way to shut down Kent's line of thinking, Kate looked at her watch. "Visiting hours were over a while ago. He's gone home. And that's for the best, honey. I know it's hard for you to see that, but it is." She'd suspected leaving at the end of their camp stay would be hard on Kent, but it was clear she'd underestimated the connection he'd made with Seb. Did they really have to get into this now, when everyone was exhausted and at the end of their ropes?

Kent frowned and got up off the couch. He went and stood by the room's windows, clearly trying to get as far away from her as he could in the small room. It was dusk, and he stared out at the darkening sky, seeming to grow dark himself. She didn't want to watch him turn back into that somber version of himself now that he'd started to emerge here. She'd held back tears the whole afternoon, and now she wasn't sure she could keep it together, even for Kent's sake.

"He's not."

Lord, I'm going to need more patience than I have right now, Kate prayed, closing her eyes and taking in a breath. "What?"

"Seb didn't go home. He's sitting out there in the parking lot looking up at us."

Seb had once thought he'd never feel a pull stronger than the one the drugs once had on him.

He was wrong.

The pull toward those three people somewhere in that hospital room was like a tidal wave. He couldn't leave. He was due back at camp, he was fully aware he needed to keep a safe distance, he was hungry and hot and his back was screaming at him, but he couldn't leave.

How can I care so much about her? About them? How is that fair? What's the point of being more broken than I already am?

From the look the reception nurse had given him when she'd informed him visiting hours were over, his pain was broadcast all over his face. She'd given him a few "mind telling me why you keep telling that boy you can't go up there when you clearly want to?" looks each of the last times Kent had come down.

"Because she needs a better man than me" seemed like the most pathetic of replies, so he never gave her looks a reply. Just sat there, holding some kind of penance vigil because he didn't know what else to do. Unable to go closer, unable to pull himself away.

From his spot in the visitors' parking lot, Seb had tried to calculate which window was Kimmy's room. He peered at each of the occupied rooms for some sign of Kate or Kent. It was probably best that he never could work it out. They could have the lights off so Kimmy could nap. They could be on the other side of the building for all he knew. What would it help if he could see the window, anyway? It had a better chance of making it that much worse.

And then, there it was. A figure Seb absolutely knew to be Kent's face peered out of one window.

Any hope that the boy didn't see him was instantly lost. The distance and glass between them disappeared when Kent's gaze met his. He could tell, even from here, that Kent was happy to see him. The boy seemed unsurprised that he was still here in the parking lot. As if waiting here was simply another version of the waiting he'd done in the lobby.

Kent gave a smile, raised his hand and waved. Seb felt the gesture flutter through every inch of his body. He couldn't have stopped himself from giving a goofy smile and waving back any more than he could have stopped the sun setting behind him. "Hey, there," he said aloud for no good reason.

Maybe the only point of him staying was just so Kent could see him right now. Maybe he was waving goodbye, and not hello. Maybe God was telling him it was time to gather his willpower and go home. Maybe…

Kate came to the window. He practically felt it before he saw her. And when he saw her, it shot through him with more voltage than a dozen of her gizmos. How could she feel right next to him and a hundred miles away at the same time? It had to be an illusion—even of his own yearning—that he felt he could see her eyes so clearly.

She put her hand up against the window, and it was as if her fingers were resting against his chest the way they had that one night. It was a full minute before he realized his own hand had come up against his chest in the vividness of the recollection.

For the first time, Seb realized an amazing thing: the longing was stronger than the pain. Like the transponders that had long since stopped working on his back, the power of his care for Kate drowned out the pain. It even came close to drowning out the fear.

Maybe...

He didn't think that would ever be possible. He wasn't even sure he could trust it. But when Kate pulled her hand from the window to beckon him to come inside, he was a hundred percent sure he was powerless to ignore it.

He blinked and looked at her, silently asking, "Really?" across the space between them. He could be imagining it. Wishing for something that wasn't really there. And he couldn't bear to get this wrong.

Kent came back into view. Kent and Kate looked at each other for a moment, and he could see them saying something to each other. Then they both turned back to the window, each of them making the "come in" gesture Seb could barely believe he was seeing.

She was asking for him, asking him to come in, to come to her. He had no doubt she was telling him she might be willing to take the step—however risky—both of them had been trying so hard to deny. It felt both impossible and inevitable at the same time.

He ought to have run. It would have made for a Hollywood moment, him barreling into the hospital and up to that room at breakneck speed. As it was, his rush into the building was more like a hobble. He was so tired and everything hurt, but Seb would have crawled over a mountain of broken glass to reach Kate and her family.

He pushed into the lobby to meet the raised eyebrows of the reception nurse. "You're back," she said with only a tiny hint of surprise.

"I never left, actually," he admitted, feeling foolish. "Couldn't. It's a long story." His heart was galloping in his chest, quickly replacing all that weariness with a pulse in anxious overdrive.

"Well, the short story is visiting hours were over forty minutes ago."

Visiting hours? Weeks of putting distance between himself and this astounding woman were going to be thwarted by *visiting hours*?

Not if he could help it. He planted his hands on the counter. "You gotta let me up there." Kate couldn't leave Kimmy. She couldn't come to him. He had to go to her. He *had* to.

"I don't have to do anything that violates procedure." Her words were stern, but there was a glow in her eyes. She wasn't totally ready to shut him down—not yet.

Seb read her name tag. "Nurse Tonisha?"

"Yes, Chef Seb?" So she'd been listening. She knew what Kent called him. Seb wondered how many of his insistent questions to Kent she'd heard. Based on her expression, she knew what was going on here. If there was ever a time to go for broke, it was now.

"Have you ever been in love?" The words jumped out of him, and within a heartbeat he knew the truth of them. He was in love with Kate Hoyle. Total, hopeless, worth-everything love. He was in love with all three of them, desperate to keep them in his life because life wouldn't be life without them. The pride that kept him out in that parking lot now seemed a massive waste. If he was a broken man, he was quite simply a far more broken man without Kate. Without all of them.

She smiled and held up her hand to show a gold band. "I have."

"Then you know why I've *got* to go up there. I've *got* to be with her. Don't you want to be the amazing person who lets that happen?"

She paused for a long moment, still smiling. "I'm supposed to ask if you're family."

The question was downright epic. "I want to be. Like you wouldn't believe."

"Oh, I believe it." Seb's chest filled with fireworks when she reached into a drawer and produced a name tag reading After Hours Visitor. When she held it out to him, he would have leaped over the counter and hugged her if he didn't think it would lay him flat for a week. "How about we leave the dictionary definition of family behind just now?" Nurse Tonisha said. "You got the look of the kind of family that really matters to me." She actually winked before she added, "Go get her."

Seb was pounding the elevator buttons before she finished her sentence.

Chapter Eighteen

The small hospital room now felt hopelessly tiny knowing Seb was on his way up here. His walking through the door meant far more than his mere arrival. It was a declaration. It was them daring to cross the line they'd both avoided, trusting that God had brought them to this wildly risky place for His reasons.

Kate twisted her fingers together, unable to control the emotions barreling through her. Fear and doubt, yes, but also a long-unfamiliar feeling: hope. A promise that maybe, just maybe, her days of scraping by alone might be coming to an end.

Kent had dashed out of the room down the hall to where the elevator was, in a hurry to meet Seb. In these few minutes alone, Kate stole a glimpse of her harried reflection in the bathroom mirror. A surge of embarrassed vanity ran through her, recalling that lush, enthralling moment when Seb had called her beautiful. She felt so far from beautiful right now. The thin, raw woman who looked back at her wasn't ready for the life-changing moment about to happen.

Then again, who was ever ready? They were about to try cobbling together the bits of incomplete lives, hoping to come up with something close to a healed whole between the two of them. *If this is as good as it gets*, she thought as she tried to smooth down her hair that seemed to stick out in all directions, *is it enough?*

It was a comfort, of sorts, that when Seb came down the corridor he looked as tottering and lost as she felt. How was it that two people could feel so much urgency and so much resistance at the same time?

"I'm here," he said, eyes steady even though he nearly fidgeted as he stood in the doorway.

"You are." Kate felt as if his gaze went through every inch of her. Had he always had such mesmerizing eyes?

"You've *been* here," Kent corrected with the kind of exasperation only a ten-year-old could produce. "Like, *the whole time*."

Kate groaned at her son's lack of tact, but Seb smirked. "Yeah, but now I'm *here* here."

She knew exactly what Seb meant. *Me, too.*

Seb glanced over at Kimmy asleep on the bed. "How is she?"

"Okay," she replied, her voice too breathy. "Resting now, at least. Everything's under control. It's just… We sort of just watch from here." Kimmy did look sweet and peaceful, a small pink form against the stark white sheets, breaths steady in the ease of sleep.

"I'm so glad she's going to be okay," Seb said, his voice catching in a way that tightened Kate's throat. "I don't know what I'd do if…" He stopped himself, as if he'd remembered Kent was in the room. He cleared his throat. "Are they always like this? The close calls?"

It would have been nice to be able to answer differently, but the moment demanded total honesty. "This one was rough, but mostly, yes."

He gave a solemn and slow nod. "Okay, then." An amazingly clear moment followed his words. Kate could see Seb lean into it. Somehow, she could literally watch him choose to put his shoulder to the yoke alongside hers. Her heart seemed to break open and expand, filling with gratitude and relief after so many months of tightly bound fear and worry. It didn't solve everything—far from it. Still, it made everything feel so much more solvable.

The air between her and Seb seemed filled with a hundred things she wanted to say to him but couldn't. How would this ever work?

His eyes still locked on hers, Seb reached into his pocket and fished out a wad of crumpled bills. "Hey, Kent, is there a vending machine in that room we passed?"

"Yeah, why?"

Seb held the bills out toward Kent. "'Cause I need to say a bunch of mushy stuff to your mom and I'm guessing you'd rather go get a candy bar than sit here and listen to it, am I right?"

Kate felt her cheeks flush. How did he do that? How did he find a way through when she couldn't see one?

Kent laughed. "Um…okay." Kate watched her son grab the money, give the two of them the most absurd look and duck out the door.

"You're horrible," she teased even as her pulse jumped.

Seb reached for her hand. "More like desperate. Kate, I…"

She kissed him. She flung herself across the line they'd drawn so firmly between them, a leap of faith that felt as gigantic as it did easy. He held her to him, and there was so much raging through his touch. It was as much fierce declaration and frightened clinging as she felt, something deep and quiet that she could never put into words. She'd never thought to find this again, to discover she could be brave enough to even dare it.

Seb caught his breath, laying one hand against her cheek while the other held her close. "Just when a guy thinks he knows how a moment's gonna go." He smiled, utter wonder lighting his eyes. "Do you know how long I've wanted to do that? And here you beat me to it."

Suddenly everything felt lighter. Not gone, or even less daunting, but lighter. "As a matter of fact, I do."

His gaze turned serious. "I don't know that I'm what you need. I want to be, but I come with a lot of baggage."

Now it was her turn to offer a solemn nod of understanding. "Okay, then."

He touched her hair, aware of what she was saying. "You deserve so much more. I'm terrified I can't be enough."

"We can be enough for each other. We're parts, you and I. With pieces missing. But I realize now that maybe the parts fit together. The four of us. Kent needs you. Kimmy needs you. And I was afraid to admit I needed you, too." She touched his jaw and watched him sway toward the contact as if it anchored him in a storm. Was that so far from the truth?

Seb brushed his lips to her forehead with an astounding tenderness. "I kept thinking my darkness stood in the way between you and me. Standing out there in the parking lot, I realized I had it wrong. It's you that stands in the way between me and my darkness. I kept asking God to send me a way through this without you. Turns out you're the way through He sent me. I know that's asking a lot, but…"

Kate cut him off. "Yes. And maybe a lot is the only thing we can ask." Finding new courage, she added, "Maybe that's what love really is. Asking a lot."

He tightened his arms around her. "Kate Hoyle, I'm pretty sure I'm in love with you. Can you live with that?"

She was astonished to feel a light eddy of laughter bubble up through her. "Pretty sure?"

"One hundred percent hopeless, actually. But I figured that was a bit much."

Kent's figure appeared in the doorway, rolling his eyes above a package of red licorice and a bag of chocolate chip cookies. "Man, you weren't kidding, were you?"

Seb pulled himself up tall, took Kate's hand and turned to look Kent straight in the eye. "I'm a hundred percent hopelessly in love with your mom. Can you live with that?"

Kent returned the look with equal directness. "Yeah, I can live with that." He shifted his gaze to her. "You, too, I guess?"

"I think so," she admitted.

One corner of Kent's mouth turned up. "Sure took you long enough."

Epilogue

August could be brutal in Arizona, but the rare eighty-degree day felt almost pleasant. Kate was grateful to walk into the church's well-working air-conditioning, but she would have gone anywhere for the occasion. She'd made three trips back to North Springs and Camp True North Springs since that first visit, so she'd seen a good sampling of Arizona summer weather.

Kimmy twirled in her frilly dress, raising her dimpled cheeks to the sunshine. "Pretty day."

Seb rushed up and caught her from behind, lofting her into the air like a fluffy white cloud in pigtails. "Pretty girl," he cooed as Kimmy giggled. He caught Kate's gaze. "Both of you." Kate felt the warm affection in his eyes even stronger than the bright glare. "You look beautiful," he said. He'd said it a hundred times since that first time, and she never tired of hearing it.

Evidently thinking he meant her, Kimmy wrapped her little arms around his neck and planted a big squishy kiss on his cheek.

"Aww," Seb said, reaching for Kate's hand. "Think I can get one of those from your mama?"

"You certainly can." Kate happily complied, letting her lips linger on Seb's jaw. Tomorrow would be the last time she'd have to say goodbye to him. In two weeks, he was flying out to Pennsylvania after the final camp session of the season to help load up a truck and move them to North Springs.

"Looking sharp there, Kent. Our fifth graders won't know what hit 'em when you get on the bus with Charlie next month."

"I forgot," Kent said with a grin. "We'll ride the same bus if we're right next door." Right after finding a job at the medical center that had been so good to Kimmy, Kate had rented a house just next to the Camp True North Springs grounds. If there had been any doubt her future could be here in North

Springs, such perfect details told her it was possible.

"How is Mason?" Kate asked. "Nervous?"

"I suppose grooms are supposed to be nervous," Seb replied. "But I'd just call him fidgety. Charlie's got him under control. Once we get him back up the mountain and the barbecue gets underway, that man's feet won't touch the ground."

The four of them began walking toward the sanctuary, beautifully decorated for Mason and Dana's wedding. They said hello to several camp families, quite a few of whom had traveled back for the occasion. As Seb wrapped his arm around Kate once they were seated in the pew, he leaned over and whispered in Kate's ear, "I'm going to have to duck out right after the ceremony to get everything underway, but make sure you come find me in the kitchen when you get on the grounds, okay?"

"Sure." Kate reveled in the way he kissed her ear, sending tingles everywhere.

"Kent," Seb said, leaning over toward the boy, "you make sure your mom heads straight to the kitchen once you get to camp, okay?"

Kent rolled his eyes. "She said sure, Seb."

"Yeah, well, you make sure her sure is sure."

"Okay."

Kate pointed to Carson Todd, the man who'd come on board as the camp's full-time groundskeeper. "Look at Carson all dressed up for the occasion." It was rare to find the man in anything but a T-shirt and jeans.

"Cleans up pretty good, doesn't he?" Seb replied. "Nice guy. Tough past. Bit of a loner." Seb winked. "Think we can change that in the coming season?"

Kate smiled. "Could be. You did say there's more staff coming on for next season. And new families."

Seb's face changed. "Two counselors and I think a nurse. And a whole new set of families—full capacity. But you all will always be the most special camp family to me."

"That's mushy," Kent declared.

"But true," Seb replied.

"Shh," Kate hushed them. "Stand up. The service is about to begin." With that, all four of them rose to watch a beaming Dana begin to make her way down the aisle toward her waiting groom. Kate felt her heart glow with happiness for those two. She owed them a great deal. She owed Camp True North

Springs for helping her find her way to healing and to hope. For bringing her the amazing man beside her.

Kate slipped her hand into Seb's as the bride walked past. Her future felt light for the first time in a long time. After all, she'd found her own true north in a second chance at true love.

It was a beautiful ceremony. Kate was gushing with happiness for Dana and Mason, as were all the guests. The camp's grounds were bursting with good cheer as the guests filed into the main house for the wedding reception and barbecue. As instructed, Kate made her way into the bustling kitchen first thing.

It was always such a pleasure to watch Seb work. He zipped around the kitchen like an orchestra conductor, organizing people, plates and scores of details. She took particular pride in how easily he could move these days. He used the TENS unit when he needed to, but it was becoming less and less often with the new exercises and treatments. Here, darting around in front of her, was the man she'd always prayed Seb could be.

When he caught sight of her, his face broke

into a wide smile. "Clear the kitchen," he announced to the handful of people pulled in to serve as waitstaff for the event.

Kate watched in amazement as they scurried from the kitchen, leaving them alone. What was he up to? There had to be dozens of tasks that needed doing—anything he had to tell her could surely wait until later in the evening.

Without a word, Seb walked over to the giant refrigerator—now covered in camp children's artwork—and opened the door. With a gleaming smile, he withdrew a spectacular-looking lemon meringue pie.

"I've owed you this for a while now. I figured tonight was a good time to pay up."

The pie he'd never made her. While he'd long since admitted it was far from his specialty, the dessert in front of her looked like a masterpiece.

Especially when she noticed what adorned the pie. Kate's heart soared at the brilliant diamond ring sitting perched on the highest peak of meringue in the center. "Seb!" she exclaimed.

He carefully picked up the ring, grinning as he wiped a tiny smear of white off the band. "Might be a bit sticky, but that's good. I want this to stay in place a good long while. Like forever."

The ring could have been covered in sticky sugar and she'd not have minded a bit.

Seb pulled her close and fixed her with a breathtaking look. "How's about I make you pie for the rest of your life? My wife should have all the pie she wants."

The smile crossing her face felt as if it could rival the stars filling the summer sky. "I like the sound of that." She looked around the kitchen. "But now? It's Mason and Dana's day."

"It was Mason's idea to do it tonight. Dana will probably aim her bouquet right at you." He kissed her, a long, luxurious kiss as if the man didn't have dozens of guests to feed. He slipped the ring onto her finger. "You're my true north. Marry me?"

"Yes." Suddenly the camp was filled with twice the happiness. Seb picked her up and spun her as easily as he had Kimmy. "Careful," she laughed as she spun. "Careful of your back."

"I feel like a million dollars tonight. Later, you and I will sneak out to the bench by the pond and dig into this pie to celebrate. What do you say?"

She grinned. "I couldn't say no to that."

"I was counting on that. Praying for that. Baking for that, actually." He slipped the pie back in the fridge and kissed her again. "Let's go tell the kids."

"They'll be over the moon," she said, slipping her hand into his.

"I was counting on that, too." And with that, they walked out of the kitchen and into the rest of their lives.

* * * * *

Dear Reader,

How quick we are to assume our lives have fallen beyond repair or beyond God's grace. And yet, He promises His grace will always be sufficient for us, and His strength is made perfect in our weakness.

Kate and Seb—and Kent and even Kimmy—teach us that the path of healing is never meant to be walked alone. Every burden is lighter when shared. I hope their story reminds you that no matter how flawed, weak or damaged you may feel, God can meet you where you are. And He can show you that you have something to offer others—even if it is simply your companionship to someone else on their journey.

If this is your first visit to Camp True North Springs, go back and learn how it all started in *A Place to Heal*, where Mason and Dana discover their own happily-ever-after. And know that future visitors to this amazing place of healing are coming your way soon.

As always, I love to hear from you. Please connect with me on Facebook, Twitter, Instagram, or my website at alliepleiter.com.

Regards,
Allie

Get 4 FREE REWARDS!

We'll send you 2 FREE Books plus 2 FREE Mystery Gifts.

FREE
Value Over
$20

Both the **Harlequin® Special Edition** and **Harlequin® Heartwarming™** series feature compelling novels filled with stories of love and strength where the bonds of friendship, family and community unite.

YES! Please send me 2 FREE novels from the Harlequin Special Edition or Harlequin Heartwarming series and my 2 FREE gifts (gifts are worth about $10 retail). After receiving them, if I don't wish to receive any more books, I can return the shipping statement marked "cancel." If I don't cancel, I will receive 6 brand-new Harlequin Special Edition books every month and be billed just $5.49 each in the U.S. or $6.24 each in Canada, a savings of at least 12% off the cover price, or 4 brand-new Harlequin Heartwarming Larger-Print books every month and be billed just $6.24 each in the U.S. or $6.74 each in Canada, a savings of at least 19% off the cover price. It's quite a bargain! Shipping and handling is just 50¢ per book in the U.S. and $1.25 per book in Canada.* I understand that accepting the 2 free books and gifts places me under no obligation to buy anything. I can always return a shipment and cancel at any time by calling the number below. The free books and gifts are mine to keep no matter what I decide.

Choose one: ☐ **Harlequin Special Edition** ☐ **Harlequin Heartwarming**
(235/335 HDN GRJV)   **Larger-Print**
                          (161/361 HDN GRJV)

Name (please print)

Address   Apt. #

City   State/Province   Zip/Postal Code

Email: Please check this box ☐ if you would like to receive newsletters and promotional emails from Harlequin Enterprises ULC and its affiliates. You can unsubscribe anytime.

Mail to the **Harlequin Reader Service:**
IN U.S.A.: P.O. Box 1341, Buffalo, NY 14240-8531
IN CANADA: P.O. Box 603, Fort Erie, Ontario L2A 5X3

Want to try 2 free books from another series! Call 1-800-873-8635 or visit www.ReaderService.com.

*Terms and prices subject to change without notice. Prices do not include sales taxes, which will be charged (if applicable) based on your state or country of residence. Canadian residents will be charged applicable taxes. Offer not valid in Quebec. This offer is limited to one order per household. Books received may not be as shown. Not valid for current subscribers to the Harlequin Special Edition or Harlequin Heartwarming series. All orders subject to approval. Credit or debit balances in a customer's account(s) may be offset by any other outstanding balance owed by or to the customer. Please allow 4 to 6 weeks for delivery. Offer available while quantities last.

Your Privacy—Your information is being collected by Harlequin Enterprises ULC, operating as Harlequin Reader Service. For a complete summary of the information we collect, how we use this information and to whom it is disclosed, please visit our privacy notice located at corporate.harlequin.com/privacy-notice. From time to time we may also exchange your personal information with reputable third parties. If you wish to opt out of this sharing of your personal information, please visit readerservice.com/consumerschoice or call 1-800-873-8635. **Notice to California Residents**—Under California law, you have specific rights to control and access your data. For more information on these rights and how to exercise them, visit corporate.harlequin.com/california-privacy.

HSEHW22R3